THE FIVE AND
THE INCA GOD

THE FIVE are Julian, Dick,
George (Georgina by rights), Anne and
Timmy the dog.

When a mysterious talking statue arrives
unexpectedly from South America at
Kirrin's antique shop, it attracts not only
the attention of the Five but also that
of some rather suspicious characters.

Why is there so much interest in this
carving, and who is behind the attempts to
steal it? The Five are soon on the trail!

Cover illustration by Peter Mennim

*Also available from Hodder Children's Books
by Claude Voilier*

The Five and the Inca God

Claude Voilier
translated by Anthea Bell

*Hodder
Children's
Books*

a division of Hodder Headline plc

British Library Cataloguing in Publication Data
Voilier, Claude
The Five And The Inca God
I. Title
843.914[J]   PZ7
ISBN 0 340 60326 7

Printed and bound in Great Britain by
Cox & Wyman Ltd, Reading, Berkshire

Hodder Children's Books
a division of Hodder Headline plc
338 Euston Road
London NW1 3BH

Contents

The Kirrin Antique Shop

'Oh, what fun to be only just starting the holidays! Don't you think so too, Timmy?'

Georgina Kirrin, who was solemnly putting this question to her dog, was dark, thin, lively, and rather tall for her age – just eleven – although anyway she would really rather have been a boy, and she was usually called George.

'Woof!' said Timmy the dog. He always agreed with everything his young mistress said! And he wagged his tail to show how pleased he was to see her. As she had said, the holidays were only just beginning. George had come home from her boarding school only the day before yesterday, and she was delighted to be back at Kirrin Cottage. It wasn't really a cottage, but quite a large house, and George, her mother and her father lived there by the sea, not far from Kirrin village.

George was an only child, and her dog Timmy

was her best friend and constant companion. He joined in all her games, and she used to talk to him just as if he was a human being. The intelligent dog seemed to understand all she said. He loved her and would follow her anywhere – everyone who lived in Kirrin knew they were inseparable!

'Just think!' George went on, running her fingers through her short, dark curls. 'More than two months of lovely summer weather here, and with Julian, Dick and Anne too! Isn't it wonderful? They'll be arriving any moment now! Oh, I feel so happy!'

And in her delight, George took Timmy's front paws and made him dance a jig with her, all the way down the garden path of Kirrin Cottage. Then she let go of him. She could hear the familiar, wheezing sound of the engine of the rattly old bus that ran between Kirrin railway station and the villages along that part of the coast. Soon it would reach the garden gate.

'Come on, Timmy, quick! It's them!' cried George. She ran to the gate, with Timmy after her. 'Here they are! Here come the others, Timmy!'

The bus stopped, and out got a tall, fair-haired boy of thirteen. He was followed by a little girl. She was fair-haired too, but she seemed to be about three years younger than her brother.

'Julian! Anne! cried George, hugging them both. 'But where's Dick?'

'Cuckoo – coming!' replied a dark-haired boy who was hauling two enormous suitcases out of the bus. 'Gosh! I'm so glad we've got here at last! It was a long journey – but hurrah for the summer holidays!'

Dick was the same age as George, and the two cousins looked rather like each other. They both had dark hair, bright eyes and mischievous smiles – and when they were both wearing jeans and T-shirts you might have taken them for brothers! George's decided manner often made people think she *was* a boy.

'George, it's good to see you!' said Julian, smiling broadly. 'And you too, of course, Timmy – how do you do?' he added, solemnly shaking the paw the dog was holding out to him.

Anne was beaming as well. 'Are Aunt Fanny and Uncle Quentin all right?' she asked her cousin. She was extremly fond of her uncle and aunt, George's parents.

'Oh yes, they're very well, and looking forward to seeing you all!' said George. 'Come indoors and say hello to them.'

Julian, Dick and Anne nearly always came to spend their holidays with George. Aunt Fanny and Uncle Quentin were delighted to have them stay, to keep their daughter company – although George's father, who was a very clever scientist, sometimes found it a nuisance having so many noisy children about the place. So the four cousins and Timmy used to spend as much time as they could out of doors. They liked that very much, so long as the weather was good!

There was a delicious tea waiting for George's cousins after their long journey. After tea, the children went out of doors to sit on the lawn and plan the things they would do these holidays. They looked forward to bathing in the sea, and going out in George's rowing boat. 'And it's always fun going for bicycle rides in the country, too,' said Julian.

'Speaking of bicycles, we ought to go and get them out!' said George. 'They've been waiting in the shed all term-time, so I bet they're terribly dusty by now.'

A little later, the four cousins were busy cleaning and oiling their bicycles, talking away nineteen to the dozen as they worked.

'By the way, there are a tremendous lot of holiday-makers staying around Kirrin this summer,' George told the others. 'We're getting quite popular with tourists here! That must be why so many antique shops are opening – there's one in almost every village now.'

'It's fashionable to furnish your house with antiques these days,' Julian explained.

'Yes, I know,' said George. 'My father told me that antique dealers can make lots of money these days, and sometimes what they're selling is only old junk! I say, did you know an antique shop has been opened in Kirrin village itself since you were last here?' And still rubbing away at her bike with an old rag, George went on to tell the others about it. 'The antique dealer's name is Barry Lane, and I've met him. Mother went to his shop yesterday to see if he had an old oil lamp. We did have one, but we've broken it – and you know how there are sometimes power failures here if there's a big storm, so it's useful to have an oil lamp in the house. Anyway, I went to the antique shop with Mother and talked to the owner. He's very nice, and he showed us all sorts of really strange and interesting things – *his* isn't a junk shop!'

'What's the difference between an antique shop and a junk shop?' asked Anne.

'Well, it just depends what sort of things they sell – whether they're worth much or not! Barry Lane has some really beautiful old furniture in his shop, and ornaments and so on. Some of it must be quite valuable. Would you like to meet him and see his shop for yourselves? We could go and call on him now – I'm sure you'd like him!'

George's cousins thought this was a good idea, and a little later the children were cycling off on their bikes to Kirrin village, followed by Timmy on foot.

George was right about the holiday-makers, as her cousins soon discovered. The village seemed much more crowded than usual.

'What a shame!' said Dick. 'I liked it better when there weren't so many people coming on holiday here!'

'But *we* like coming here for *our* holidays, Dick!' Anne pointed out gently.

'Yes,' said Julian, laughing. 'Anne's right – she was too kind to say so, but you shouldn't be a dog in the manger, Dick!'

'Woof, woof' barked Timmy.

'That's all right, Timmy, old chap – nobody was calling *you* a dog in the manger!' Julian told him, laughing.

There was quite a crowd in Barry Lane's shop. The sign over the door said ANTIQUES, in big letters, so that you could see it some way off. George and her cousins joined the passers-by who were pressing their noses to the glass of the shop window. It was full of small pieces of furniture, and vases and ornaments. Anybody ought to have been able to find something to their taste there!

'Come on, let's go in,' suggested George. 'Barry's very friendly – and a great talker! He told me he was only in Kirrin for the tourist season, and his shop here won't be open all the year round. He really lives in London and runs an antiques business there with a partner.'

When a group of customers came out of the crowded shop, the children seized their opportunity to make their way in. Barry Lane was talking to some people who were obviously wondering whether or not to buy something. He was a man of about thirty, tall and fair, with a cheerful smile and a twinkle in his eyes.

'Yes,' he was assuring his customers. 'That table really is genuine Queen Anne! What about the woodworm holes, did you say? Oh, they're genuine Queen Anne too – made by genuine Queen Anne woodworms. All dead and gone now, like Queen Anne herself, but who knows? You might find some genuine Queen Anne fossilised woodworms inside! And what more could you want, at the price?'

That made the customers laugh. It really *was* a pretty little table they were looking at, and they decided to buy it. After that, Barry Lane sold two little china ornaments, and then the children found themselves alone in the shop with him. The antique dealer recognised George and said hello, and she introduced her cousins to him.

'I liked your sales talk, Mr Lane!' said Julian, smiling.

'Just call me Barry!' said the antique dealer, smiling back. 'It's not so formal! My sales talk? Well, it's not difficult to get the trick of it! I've found out that you're more likely to sell something if you can make your customers laugh!'

The children and Barry Lane took to each other at once. It turned out that the antique dealer really knew a lot about his trade, and he was enthusiastic about the shop. He proudly showed the children several pretty things. There was a statuette of a graceful dancer in a ballet dress standing on top of a musical box – Barry wound up the clockwork which made her do a little curtsey, specially for Anne. Julian admired some old armour hanging on the walls, and Dick started playing with an old backgammon board. As for George, she gazed, fascinated, at a beautiful model of an old-fashioned sailing ship. It was an unusual curio, and Barry evidently thought a lot of it, so he was pleased to see how much George liked it too.

In fact, the children were quite surprised when they looked at their watches and saw how fast the time had been passing – it was half past five, and Barry was going to shut up shop for the day. They gave him a cheerful wave as they said goodbye, promising to come back and visit him another day, and then they set off for Kirrin Cottage on their bicycles.

After their visit to the antique shop, the children paid Barry several more calls. They were in Kirrin village almost every day, and they nearly always found time to drop in and see their new friend. Timmy liked him too – Barry always seemed to have a sugar lump in his pocket for the dog!

'I'm so glad you've come to Kirrin,' Anne told the antique dealer one day, in her shy little voice.

'It's never boring here – you tell such funny stories, and you're never cross!'

'I have plenty of other faults, I'm afraid!' said Barry, laughing. 'My business partner tells me I'm hopeless at keeping the records straight. He's stayed in London, running our shop there, while I came down here to open this one for the summer. My trouble is that I'm always losing important papers, and I can never think what I've done with them. If I had to run the business on my own I'm afraid I'd soon be broke – even though I *do* know what I'm talking about when it comes to antiques themselves!' he added with a grin.

Altogether, the first week of the holidays passed very enjoyably – and then, one day as the children were out in the garden, George remarked out loud, to nobody in particular, 'You know, there's something not quite right. Here we are together again – all the Five! The Five who have such exciting adventures! The Five who solve difficult problems! The amazing, one and only Famous Five! And there's not the faintest whiff of a mystery or an adventure for us this time – it's not fair!'

Julian couldn't help laughing.

'Don't be so impatient, George!' he told his cousin. 'Here we are, with the holidays hardly started yet, and you expect us to be up to our necks in some thrilling adventure already! Adventures don't just spring up out of the ground when you want them to, you know!'

George, who was sitting on the grass, put her arm round Timmy's neck.

'I don't see why *not*, Ju!' she said. 'I mean, when the Five are together like this, we nearly always *do* have exciting adventures, so why should't we this time? We *ought* to have an adventure – after all, we've had plenty of practice! We're a positively brilliant team when it comes to solving mysteries!'

'My word, aren't you modest?' Dick teased his cousin.

'You be quiet, Dick!' said Anne, very unexpectedly. 'You know George is right – at least as far as *she's* concerned! She's the one who gets really clever ideas when we're trying to solve a puzzling problem.'

'Thanks, Anne,' said George, feeling rather touched by her timid little cousins's standing up for her like this, 'but we *all* get clever ideas! We make a fine *team* of detectives, as I was saying!'

'Though what's the use of a team of detectives without any mystery to solve?' asked Dick, nodding gloomily in agreement with George.

'Oh, do stop it, all of you!' said Julian lazily. 'Let's just enjoy our holidays – bathing and playing games and so on. If there *is* going to be an adventure these holidays, it'll find its own way to us, don't worry!'

And the four cousins and Timmy jumped up and started to play a lively game of hide-and-seek, forgetting about adventures for the time being.

But Julian was soon to be proved right!

2

The Bolivian Statue

Poor George – she couldn't bear being bored, and after a week of the holidays she began to feel it *was* boring, with nothing to do but play, eat and sleep. One morning, however, a couple of days after their conversation in the garden, the four cousins were all talking cheerfully over breakfast. Uncle Quentin, who was always in a hurry to get back to his work, soon got up from the table and went to shut himself away in his study for the morning. He had been glancing quickly through the newspaper, and he left it on the breakfast table, beside his plate. Julian picked it up, and to amuse the others he started reading aloud some bits of local news, adding funny comments of his own! Then he came upon a little news item which he thought was really interesting.

'I say!' he exclaimed. 'Just listen to this – it's about Kirrin! Apparently there's a most unusual

Bolivian wooden statue on sale at an antique shop in the village.'

'Oh, most antique shops have wooden statues in them,' said George. 'I don't see what's so unusual or interesting about that!'

'That's because you didn't let me finish!' Julian pointed out. 'There *is* something interesting about this particular statue – jolly interesting, too! It talks!'

'A *talking* statue?' said Anne, astonished.

'Don't get all excited, Anne!' Dick told his sister in rather a patronising way. 'I expect it works by clockwork, or something like that.'

Julian smiled. 'Even if it *does* work by clockwork, the statue still sounds interesting,' he said. 'The newspaper goes on to say it's almost life-size!'

George did seem intrigued now. 'We could go and take a look at it,' she said. 'Why not?'

'We don't know just where it is, do we?' said Anne.

'Yes, we do – the papers say an antique shop in Kirrin, and there's only one antique shop, it must be at Barry Lane's.'

'Oh, good!' said Anne, sounding pleased. 'I'm sure he'll let us have a really good look at it!'

'*And* have a conversation with it too, I expect!' added Dick. 'Golly – suppose it's the statue of another little girl who chatters away like you! There'll be no stopping the pair of you!'

Anne knew Dick was only teasing, so she didn't lose her temper, but just laughed. She was a very sweet-natured little girl, who got on well with everyone. The excitable George was like dynamite beside her cousin! But Julian was calmer and more easy-going, like his little sister – he was the most sensible of the children, as well as being the eldest.

'Right!' he said. 'We might as well go to the shop this morning – if we leave it till later, the statue may be sold by the time we get there.'

Once they were on their bicycles, making for the village, the children all began to wonder just what the strange talking statue could be like. How would it look? What was it a statue *of*? And most interesting of all, how on earth did it talk? They really couldn't imagine!

When the four cousins reached Barry's shop, they got off their cycles and hurried in. Luckily there weren't any customers yet at this time of the morning, and Barry welcomed his visitors with a smile.

'Hello – it's the five from Kirrin Cottage again!' he said cheerfully. 'Good morning, all of you! And what brings *you* here so early?'

'It's this story we read in the paper,' explained Julian, holding out the page headed 'Regional News' to the antique dealer. 'It's about a talking statue, and – '

'Oh, and you've come to buy it?' asked Barry, jokingly.

'So it *is* here in your shop!' cried Anne.

'Yes, it is – and I can tell you're longing to see it. It's a very fine statue, too.'

Barry led the children into the room at the back of the shop. A tall, dark form seemed to be standing guard there.

'I was just polishing it up a bit before I put it on display,' Barry explained.

'But if it wasn't on display already, how did the newspaper reporter know it was here?' asked Dick, puzzled.

'Oh, that's easy!' said Barry. 'I told them, of course! I thought they'd be interested, and maybe give me a nice bit of free publicity, so I telephoned to tell them about the statue. The newspaper report ought to bring plenty of tourists into the shop. Now, how about lending me a hand to get this gentleman through into the front?'

Julian and Dick helped carry the 'gentleman' from the room at the back and into the main part of the shop. Now they could see the statue in a good light they could admire all the details.

'It's made of carved wood,' Barry told them, 'and it looks to me as if it's meant to be some primitive god. The crate it came in was sent from La Paz in Bolivia. It just turned up here, quite unexpectedly – and as there wasn't a bill on the crate, or any other documents, I suppose my partner Alan must have bought it and had it sent straight to me here.

When I get a moment, I must write and tell him it's arrived, but I don't expect there's any hurry. It must have taken weeks to reach England, so a few more days won't matter!'

George was examining the statue from all sides. It was the size of a man – not a very large man, but all the same, it was an impressive sight. It had a dignified-looking face, with a high forehead, thin nose and large eyes.

'Have you noticed, it's sort of hollow behind?' she said. 'Isn't that funny! I've never seen anything quite like it before.'

'Nor have I,' Dick agreed. 'It's like a huge mask that would reach from head to foot of anyone standing behind it.'

'And that's not the only unusual thing about it,' said Barry mysteriously.

'Oh yes – it talks!' Julian remembered.

'That's right. Like to try it, then?'

'How?' asked Anne, her eyes shining with interest. 'Do you press a button, like the buttons on talking dolls, or what?'

'No!' said Barry, laughing. 'And there's no clockwork, or tape recording or anything modern like that inside my statue! I'll give you a demonstration. Julian, you're the tallest – you come over here. Stand behind the statue and move close to the hollow part. Your lips should be at about the level of the idol's mouth. Now say something –

anything – but very quietly. You get the idea? Go on, try it!'

Doing as Barry had said, and almost whispering, Julian announced, 'Bow down, everyone! I am the king of all the Bolivian gods!'

Then George, Dick and Anne, who were standing right in front of the statue, uttered exclamations of astonishment! The god himself seemed to be speaking, in a voice like thunder!

Timmy, who had been sniffing the statue suspiciously, leaped into the air, ears back and coat bristling, and landed on all four paws again with a howl of terror. George, Dick and Anne exchanged puzzled glances. They didn't understand how the loud voice had been produced.

Seeing them look so baffled, Barry burst out laughing. 'Dear me, if you could only see your faces! Surprised you, did it? You must admit, the god has a good pair of lungs! You only have to whisper – and because it's like a mask, the statue amplifies the sound and makes it tremendously loud. It's like a megaphone – and even in these modern times you wouldn't find one that worked any better.'

Poor Anne was still feeling rather frightened and bewildered. 'But what *was* it?' she gasped. 'Where did that dreadful voice come from?'

'It was only Julian, Anne,' Barry explained, realising that she hadn't taken in his explanation.

'I see!' said George excitedly. 'It's a sort of –

acoustic effect known as long ago as the days of
ancient Greece. I know because our history teacher
at school was telling us about the actors in those
days, and how they used the same sort of idea in their
performances – they put masks over their faces to
make their voices louder, and project them all over
the open-air theatres where plays were acted.'

'Oh yes, that's right!' agreed Dick. '*We* learnt
about that at school last term, too! It meant the
audience could hear what was being said even if
they were sitting in the very back rows, a long way
from the stage.'

'We're more up-to-date nowadays,' said Julian,
emerging from behind the statue. 'We use loud-
speakers and microphones instead of masks! All
the same, that statue does have an amazing range
of sound.'

'That's what makes it such an interesting curio,'
said Barry. 'I think it's very old, too, so I shall be
able to get a good price for it.'

Now it was George's turn to slip inside the hollow
back of the wooden statue. If she stood on tip-toe,
she could just manage to get her mouth level with
the god's.

'Timmy! Timmy!' she whispered.

Amplified over and over again, the sound made
the glass of Barry's shop window shake! Timmy,
who knew his own name, leaped up in the air again,
squealing like a pig with somebody treading on its

tail. Barry and the children burst out laughing – and as George was still inside the hollow statue, her own laughter sounded like a tremendous roll of drums. Poor Timmy was panic-stricken. He shot off like an arrow, round to the other side of the statue, and flung himself on George as if he were asking her to protect him.

'Woof! Woof!' he barked.

Seeing that Timmy was inside the huge 'mask' himself now, Barry, Julian, Dick and Anne witnessed the unusual sight of a dignified Bolivian god barking at them frantically! The children laughed so much they were quite out of breath, and so was Barry. George, however, felt rather sorry she had frightened her darling Timmy, and coaxed him out of hiding behind the statue.

'There, there, Timmy – come on! Good dog! Don't worry, it's only a silly old bit of wood!'

Timmy soon calmed down, just as if he understood what she was saying, but he was looking very embarrassed. Usually, he was such a brave dog when faced with any danger – but he'd let that terrible, loud voice scare him out of his wits! The poor creature was very cross with himself.

When Barry could at last stop laughing, he told the children more about idols like this Bolivian god, and said he thought it was likely the statue had been used in religious ceremonies at the time of the Incas.

He would have told them more, but some customers came in to look at the statue. They had been attracted by all the noise in the shop! Barry immediately launched into his 'sales talk', pointing out all the Bolivian god's remarkable qualities.

The children didn't want to get in his way, so they left. But they kept talking about the wooden statue, and the strange effect you got by speaking through its mouth, and they were eager to see it again when they called to see Barry in his shop next day, as usual.

As soon as they turned the corner of the road, and came in sight of the antique shop, Dick exclaimed, 'Oh, look! Barry's put the statue out on the pavement, beside his door!'

'I expect that's to bring in customers,' said George.

'You'd have to be very rich to buy a valuable antique like that,' said Julian. 'So let's hope Barry's lucky, and he soon gets a very, *very* rich customer, who's mad about Bolivian art!'

'Is Bolivia the country that the Incas used to rule?' Anne asked.

'Yes, that's right,' George told her. 'The Inca Empire was made up of what is now Bolivia and Peru. Inca was a word meaning "king", and the Inca's people worshipped him like a god – though they had other gods too, like the one represented by Barry's statue, I expect.'

A number of curious onlookers had gathered round the wooden statue. Now and then someone more daring than the rest would get behind it and say a few words through the mask's wooden mouth. Anything he said was immediately amplified many times over – and the noise attracted more passers-by to swell the sound. How clever of Barry! That was just what he wanted.

'I don't think we ought to bother Barry when he's so busy,' said Julian, who was very thoughtful about other people. 'We'll come back tomorrow.'

'Meanwhile, why don't we think of a name for the statue?' suggested George. 'It ought to have an Inca-sounding sort of name – how about Chocabloc? When somebody stands behind him he *is* choc-a-block – full of human being!'

Anne laughed. 'That's a good name!' she said. 'And it sounds quite Peruvian or Brazilian too!'

'Central American, anyway,' said Dick. 'I read somewhere that the rain god of ancient Mexico was called Tlaloc.'

'Chocabloc it is, then!' said Julian.

The next day the children told Barry the name George had invented, and he laughed with his usual good humour. 'I agree – Chocabloc's a fine name for him!' he said. 'I hope he likes it!'

Chocabloc was still attracting a lot of attention. The summer holiday-makers who came to see him talked and joked about him – but they all discovered he cost far too much for them to buy. All the same, that didn't stop them going into Barry Lane's shop and coming away with smaller and cheaper souvenirs of their visit to Kirrin.

'As a matter of fact, I don't know that I *want* to sell Chocabloc just yet,' Barry told the children. 'I expect I'll find a rich buyer quite easily when I go back to London at the end of the tourist season. And meanwhile, he's making himself very useful here, fetching in customers who don't have so much money to spend, but will still buy something small. I think I'll hang on to him for a little longer.'

It was two days later that George and her cousins looked in at the shop to say hello to their friend – and for once they found the antique dealer looking very glum. This was so unusual that they couldn't help asking what the matter was.

'Oh, never mind!' snapped Barry. Then he said, apologetically, 'Sorry, I'm in a bad mood, but it's not *your* fault! You know, I'm usually an easy-going sort – but I can be really obstinate and dig my heels in if I feel like it, and it's just too bad if anyone gets me annoyed then!'

'But what's happened?' asked George, bewildered. 'Who's been annoying you?'

'A stranger who came into the shop – foreign, I think,' said Barry. 'At least, he had a Spanish accent. He wanted to buy Chocabloc, and when I told him I'd decided not to sell the statue yet, he was so keen to have it, I almost thought he'd carry it off by force!'

'My word!' said Dick. 'Honestly?'

'Well, maybe I'm exaggerating a little bit, but he certainly didn't want to take no for an answer! I explained that the statue makes an unusual advertisement and brings in the customers, so he wasn't for sale at the moment, but he wouldn't listen.'

'Obstinate, just like you?' said George, smiling.

'He certainly was! "Name your own price and I'll pay it," he kept saying. Actually, I think it was his self-satisfied tone of voice I didn't like,' said Barry. 'He was so sure I'd sell him the statue – in the end I practically threw him out of the shop. Once I do start to lose my temper, the more people argue with me the angrier I get!'

Barry was telling his story in such a comical way that the children could hardly help laughing – but they could see he really *was* upset. Anne, who always felt sympathetic to other people, was quite worried when she saw his face go red with anger again as he described what had happened.

'Never mind, Barry – please don't get so worked up!' she said kindly. 'Why don't I make you a nice cup of tea?'

That was thoughtful of her – Barry was very fond of tea, and the children knew there was nearly always a kettle on the boil in the room behind the shop! So Anne led him off with her to make a pot of tea. George, Dick and Julian followed them. In a little while, Barry calmed down, and soon he was laughing at himself for letting a silly thing like a troublesome customer upset him!

Then, suddenly, the door bell of the shop rang.

'A customer!' said Barry, getting to his feet. They had left the door into the shop ajar, and he glanced through it. Then he exclaimed, in a low voice, 'Oh no! It's him again!'

3

A Popular Idol

'Him? Who?' asked George.

'Why, that man who was ready to buy Chocabloc at any price I cared to name!' said Barry angrily. 'I've had enough of *him* – you just wait a minute and I'll send him packing!'

He went into the shop, to attend to his unwanted customer. The four cousins looked through the doorway themselves, and saw a very elegant-looking man standing there. He was tall and thin, with black hair and a neat little moustache, and he gave Barry a big smile.

'I'm so sorry to bother you again!' he said. He spoke perfect English, but with a slight foreign accent – Barry had said it was Spanish, the children remembered. 'However, I really felt I had to come back – I'm simply haunted by the thought of that statue of yours! You see, it's exactly the kind of thing my wife wants to stand in the hall of our house. I've

been searching for a statue like it for so long, and it
would really be perfect!'

'Maybe,' said Barry, rather brusquely. 'But I've
already told you, it's not for sale.'

'Listen – I know it *was* for sale, only a few days
ago! Exactly what were you asking for it then?'

'A thousand pounds!' said Barry – and the children gasped.

'I'll give you double,' said the foreigner. The
children gasped again! 'I want to give my wife a
birthday present she'll really like, and I've decided
that your Inca statue is just the thing!'

'And *I've* decided not to sell it!' growled Barry.
'When I've made a decision, I don't go back on it
just because somebody offers me a higher price!'

The two men went on arguing for several minutes.
Barry looked very much as if he were going to lose
his temper again. Finally, he marched to the shop
door and held it wide open.

'We're both of us wasting our time,' he told his
would-be customer. 'So don't let me keep you!'

The other man couldn't do anything but walk
out, narrowing his lips as he went. George and her
cousins had taken care to stay in the background,
but now they came out of the room behind the shop
to join their friend – and Anne thoughtfully handed
him another cup of steaming hot tea!

'Thanks, Anne,' said Barry gratefully, sipping it.
'Well – I hope you heard how I dealt with that

fellow! Infuriating! I don't like it when people try to be funny with me. The statue is worth a thousand pounds – but fancy offering *two* thousand for it! It's not worth anything like *that* much! A poor sort of joke, if you ask me!'

But George was frowning. 'I wonder if it really *was* a joke?' she said quietly. 'That man sounded perfectly serious to me, Barry!'

'Yes, George is right,' Julian agreed. '*I* don't think he was being funny – he didn't hesitate for a moment before offering you all that money for the statue. He looked rich, too. Maybe you ought to have accepted.'

But the antique dealer was obviously still feeling annoyed, and he shook his head. 'You may be right there!' he admitted. 'I know I can be very pig-headed . . . all the same, just *why* was he so keen to have the statue at any price?'

Dick and George were examining their now familiar friend Chocabloc as if they'd never set eyes on him before.

'Perhaps the idol really *is* worth two thousand pounds?' suggested Dick.

'It's an unusual curio, all right,' agreed Barry, 'but let me tell you, I know my job! Two thousand pounds would be a ridiculous price! Unless, of course, there's something else unusual about the statue – something I haven't discovered yet!'

The children watched with great interest as Barry

examined Chocabloc from the toes of his bare feet
to the carved wooden feathers he wore on top of his
head – but none of them could see anything new
about the statue.

'No, I'm sure of it now!' Barry said. 'That man
was either a practical joker or a lunatic!'

George and her cousins were not so sure, but
they could tell it was no use trying to persuade
Barry he might be wrong. They went off to do
some shopping for Aunt Fanny in the village, and
then spent the rest of that afternoon playing on
the beach.

Next day, they went for a long bicycle ride into
the country, taking a picnic with them, and they
were out all day. As they were going to bed that
evening, Anne said, 'We'd better go and see Barry
tomorrow, or he'll think we're not friends with him
any more!'

'Gosh, yes – we've really been spoiling him,
going to see him almost every day!' said George,
smiling.

'I expect he was terribly sad not to see us yesterday!' agreed Dick, with a grin. 'Still, who knows –
perhaps that man who wanted to buy the statue so
much came back to cheer him up!'

It was about the middle of the morning when the
children and Timmy went off to Kirrin village next
day. They left their bicycles beside the road, and
were just going into the shop when Julian took a

look through the window first. 'Barry's busy with a customer,' he said. 'We'd better wait.'

'I say – he looks annoyed again, too!' said Dick softly. 'There's thunder in the air!'

The door of the shop wasn't quite shut. George went up to it and peered through the crack. She saw the antique dealer arguing with big, tall man, who had a rugged sort of face and was wearing a bright check shirt. He looked just like her idea of one of the old Wild West pioneers.

'Whew!' whistled Dick, admiringly. 'See those muscles? And the width of his shoulders? He could easily be a film star in a cowboy picture! And look – Barry's going red as a lobster again! I wonder what's up?'

The children only just had time to move away from the shop door as the 'cowboy' came storming out, looking as angry as Barry himself. He didn't even seem to see them as he passed, shouting furiously, 'Well, if you won't sell, you can just keep your stupid statue!'

'I will, too!' shouted Barry, just as angrily. 'I'm sick and tired of saying I don't want to part with it yet!'

The big man in the check shirt marched off, muttering to himself, and Barry saw the children.

'Hello there!' he said. 'Well – Chocabloc is certainly what you might call a popular idol! Guess what? That great hunk who's just gone out wanted

him too, and what do you think he offered me?
As a matter of fact, you never *would* guess. *Three*
thousand pounds! It's incredible!'

George was frowning. 'It's certainly very odd!'
she said. 'You told us that the other man's offer
was ridiculous, and here's an even higher one! That
elegant-looking man with the Spanish accent might
really have wanted to give his wife a handsome,
unusual sort of present – but your customer just
now didn't look much like an art-lover. He didn't
look very rich, either.'

'You're right there,' Barry told her. 'I'm assuming
that Customer Number One, our friend with the
Spanish accent, knew it was no good turning up
again himself – so he sent Customer Number Two
to act on his behalf! Well, if they think I'm selling
them my statue, they can think again! I know it's
a lot of money to turn down, but when I say no I
mean no!' Suddenly Barry burst out laughing. 'Oh,
dear – I lost my temper again!' he said ruefully. The
children were glad to see he was his old, cheerful self
again. 'What luck my partner Alan isn't here!' he
added. 'He'd think I was mad to turn down two
such offers!'

George felt both worried and excited – worried
on Barry's account, because she felt sure there was
some shady reason behind the two men's attempts
to buy the statue, excited because she had an idea
the Five were on the point of finding an adventure

again! Rather an exotic adventure, too. 'We could call it the Mystery of the Inca God!' she thought to herself.

Timmy was sniffing all round Chocabloc again. 'You'd think Timmy suspected there was something funny about that idol too!' said Barry, watching him. 'I wonder what can make him seem so valuable? Well, all things considered, I'm glad I didn't sell him – Alan and I will get an expert opinion about him back in London, and we can always sell him then. I still feel there must be something about the statue I've missed seeing!'

'You know,' Julian ventured to suggest, 'if I were you, Barry, I wouldn't go leaving him out on the pavement outside the shop door like that!'

But Barry only laughed, quite carefree again now. 'Oh, he's much too heavy for any thief just to pick him up and walk away with him! He's not like a ring or a snuffbox – the sort of thing you can stuff into a pocket to hide it!'

Anne and the boys laughed, too, but George didn't. She was thinking hard. She had a strong suspicion that no antique expert's opinion would ever reveal the secret of Chocabloc – supposing the statue really did hold a secret that made it very valuable.

That evening she said so to her cousins, in the garden of Kirrin Cottage, 'I'm *sure* there's a mystery of some kind about that idol!' she finished. 'Those two amazing offers Barry's customers made can't have been simply a joke!'

'I agree – I don't think so either,' said Julian.

'Nor do I,' said Dick.

'And I don't either,' added Anne.

'Woof!' said Timmy, not to be left out.

George was looking very determined. 'We must keep our ears and eyes wide open from now on!' she told the others. 'I wouldn't be a bit surprised if something else happens soon, and we must be ready to act if Barry needs our help! All right?'

'All right!' said her cousins, in chorus.

'Woof!' agreed Timmy once again.

Thursday was market day in Kirrin. The village people, and people from the countryside around, all came to buy and sell, and in summer there was an even bigger crowd than usual, because of tourists looking round for souvenirs to buy. So the market was very busy! The children enjoyed strolling round the stalls, looking at all the things on sale. Anne thought it would be nice to take Aunt Fanny some flowers, and bought a bunch. George had a look at some old books on a second-hand book stall. Dick bought himself a new penknife, and Julian listened with interest to a couple of farmers bargaining over the price of a cow. Later on, when they were feeling a bit tired, they went to the tea-shop. It was so warm that there were tables with umbrellas over them out on the pavement, and the children sat there eating delicious strawberry ice cream.

They could see Barry's antique shop from where they were sitting, and they noticed a lot of customers going in. Then people began to drift away from the market stalls, and the stallholders began to shut up shop. Some of them had a long way to go before they reached home that evening.

When George and her cousins thought Barry's customers had all left too, they paid for their ice cream and went off to see him. There was their old friend Chocabloc still on guard at the door of the shop, looking very grand and impressive.

The very moment the Five walked into the shop, the telephone bell rang. Barry smiled at the children, and waved apologetically to show he couldn't talk to them just now, and picked up the phone, which was on the shop counter. 'Hello?' he said. 'Police, did you say? Yes . . . yes, that's me . . .'

George was watching the antique dealer, and she saw an expression of consternation spread over his face.

'What . . . *what* did you say?' he exclaimed. 'Me? I ran down a child with my van? But that's nonsense – I never did any such thing! *What*? I failed to report the accident, you say? A case of hit-and-run driving? . . . This is ridiculous! I'd never . . . you want me to account for my movements? Well, listen, this story is quite crazy, but if as you say the accident occurred between five and six in Fisherman's Lane, I've got an alibi. I didn't leave my shop all day! . . . What? . . . Yes, I *have* got witnesses to prove it! . . . No, I tell you I didn't even get my van out of the garage yesterday!'

Of course, George and her cousins couldn't tell exactly what the person at the other end of the line was saying to Barry, but they couldn't help hearing *his* side of the conversation, and it was perfectly clear what it was about.

'You want me to come to the police station straightaway . . . you think that's the best way to clear the matter up? But my shop . . . oh very well, I'll fix something. But of all the stupid stories . . . yes, all right, I'm on my way! Just give me time to shut the shop!'

Barry put the receiver down. He looked puzzled and horrified at the same time.

'Did you ever hear anything like it?' he said, turning to the children. 'What a dreadful thing to happen! The police think I ran down a little boy, and then drove off without stopping to see what had happened to my victim or reporting the accident! Of course it's all a stupid mistake, but I have to go straight off to the police station to explain what I was doing yesterday. Oh, what appalling luck!'

Poor Barry! The children knew he couldn't have done what he was accused of, but he was obviously shattered by the mere idea of it. And as he hadn't been in Kirrin very long, he didn't even know where to find the police station. The Kirrin police had recently moved into a new building a little way outside the village, and it wasn't easy to explain the way, so the children offered to go with him.

Barry scratched his head. 'Well – the fact is, there's something else I was going to ask you to do for me!' he said. 'It's a real nuisance having to close the shop early on a market day – I was wondering if you'd stay here and ask any customers to wait until I come back? There might be some late-comers, and I wouldn't want to miss a possible sale! I don't expect the police will keep me long.'

George thought fast. 'I tell you what – the others can go with you,' she said. 'It'll be much easier for you to find the new police station with someone to show you the way, and meanwhile I'll stay here and look after the shop for you, with dear old Timmy to help me. So don't worry – everything will be quite all right!'

Barry gratefully accepted her offer, and he, Julian, Dick and Anne got into his station wagon and drove off.

— 4 —

George's Adventure

George stood in the doorway of the antique shop, watching the station wagon disappear round the corner of the next road. She patted Timmy, who was standing beside her.

'So we're left to mind the shop!' she told the dog. 'Well, *I'm* quite happy – it gives me a chance to take a really good look at old Chocabloc! It's a pity Barry left him out on the pavement, though.'

But George didn't have time to put this plan of hers into action. A possible customer was already approaching her – and much to her surprise she recognised the dark-haired man with the foreign accent who had been so keen to buy the Bolivian god a couple of days before! She wasn't quite sure why, but she suddenly decided he must be not Spanish but South American, like Chocabloc himself. He didn't even seem to notice George, he was staring so hard at the wooden statue.

'Good afternoon, sir,' said George, politely. 'Can I help you? Mr Lane has had to go out for a few moments, but he'll be back soon. Would you like to come inside the shop and wait for him?'

The stranger frowned for a moment, and then smiled. 'Good afternoon, young man!' he said. Like so many other people, he thought George was a boy! 'Well – yes, I'll come in. I'd like to look at – at those pretty antique brooches you have in the window. They look rather interesting.'

George was delighted. The brooches had price tickets on them, so she would know what to ask, and Barry would be pleased if she sold one. She'd been afraid, for a moment, that she was going to have to argue about Chocabloc, but the foreigner must have given up hope of buying the statue after all.

'Certainly, sir,' she said, taking the box of silver brooches out of the window. 'Take your pick.'

The 'South American' glanced at the brooches, picked one up and held it out to George. 'I'll have this one,' he said.

'That will be two pounds fifty,' said George, rather pleased with herself.

'Fine! Here's a ten-pound note – I'm afraid I haven't got anything smaller.'

And George hadn't got any change! She herself had asked Barry to lock the till before he left, because she thought that would be the safest thing to do. However, she didn't hesitate for long. Timmy

could perfectly well guard the shop while she ran
over to the teashop and got change for the note.
Mrs Brown, who kept the teashop, was a friend of
hers and was sure to help.

'I'll have to go and get change,' she told the man.
'Er – if you don't mind, don't touch anything while
I'm gone!' she added, rather apologetically. 'I know
it would only be out of interest, but my dog would
go for you if he saw you do it!'

The man smiled. 'I'll wait outside!' he said, following George out into the road and closing the glass
door of the shop behind him. 'That sounds safer!'

George ran off – but when she had reached the
middle of the market place, where people were
taking down their stalls, she stopped short. She'd
suddenly thought of something.

'Suppose there *is* something shady about that
man, after all?' she said to herself. 'And suppose
he gave me a ten-pound note to change on purpose
to get me away from the shop? He did seem to want
Chocabloc so much – he might well be prepared to
steal him.'

But then she remembered how heavy the statue
was. That reassured her. As Barry had said to Julian,
Chocabloc wasn't the kind of small object you could
just slip into your pocket.

All the same, something made her turn round.
She took cover behind a barrow, loaded up with
green plants and pots of flowers, so that she could

see without being seen. And what she *did* see rooted her to the spot! Her 'South American' wasn't just standing idly waiting for his change outside the antique shop. He seemed to be in a great hurry about something, and was waving impatiently. Following the direction of his gestures, George saw a truck parked not very far away.

She remembered noticing the truck among a number of other vehicles that had been standing near the market stalls that afternoon – not many people would have done so, but George was very observant. In fact, it was just *because* the truck looked so anonymous that she had specially noticed it! It was grey and ordinary-looking, not very old or very new, with a number plate which was so dirty it was hard to make out what it said. In fact it wasn't a noticeable sort of vehicle at all.

It was reversing down the road now, and it stopped just outside Barry's shop. The driver jumped out. George bit back an exclamation. It was the big, tall man in the bright shirt, the one Dick had said looked like a film star in a cowboy picture!

'So Barry was right!' said George to herself. 'The South American and the cowboy are accomplices, and they're still after Chocabloc! Oh, I ought to have suspected! That foreign man just wanted an excuse to get me out of the way! I expect if his trick of giving me a large note to change hadn't worked, he'd have thought of something else. And now he's going off with the statue, with the other man's help. Well, I'm not letting them get away with this!'

George was simply furious to think how she had been tricked! She started running back along the road the way she had come. Somehow, she must stop the two men going off with the statue of the Inca god – and there was no time to lose! The men were already picking Chocabloc up. They could lift him quite easily between them, and they were putting him in the back of their truck. The tailboard was down, ready for him. George clenched her fists and ran faster.

'I ought to be able to stop them leaving, with Timmy to help me,' she thought. 'And then we'll see what we will see!'

But what she saw, unfortunately, was – stars! Hurtling forward at top speed, poor George stumbled over an empty crate and fell, knocking against a little barrow of apples that hadn't been sold. The barrow rocked, and the fruit tumbled to the ground.

'Watch out, boy!' shouted the woman with the barrow. George was rubbing herself and looking rueful. 'Can't you look where you're going?'

'I – I'm awfully sorry,' stammered George, very cross with herself. 'I – I stumbled and fell, I didn't mean to . . .'

Hearing her voice, the woman realised she was speaking to a little girl and not a boy, and a polite little girl too. 'Well, never mind, my dear!' she said in a much kinder voice. 'The apples aren't quite ripe yet, so there won't be many bruised.'

George had been afraid she'd have to waste a lot of time apologising to the woman. She said thank you with relief, and started running again. But she had already lost too much time after all! She had a sinking feeling that she was going to get to the antique shop too late. The 'cowboy' was already behind the wheel of the truck, the 'South American' was sitting beside him, the tailboard of the truck was up again and the engine was running. Yes – the two men were about to leave, taking the Inca statue with them.

George felt her heart thudding hard as she gasped for breath. She still had a little way to go. 'This can't happen. I won't *let* it happen!' she kept telling herself as she put on a last spurt.

At last she reached the antique shop. On the other side of the glass door, Timmy seemed to have guessed there was something wrong. He was barking and jumping up and down. George thought how clever the dark-haired man had been, making sure her dog was shut *inside* the shop when they came out.

'It's too late for me to do anything about that now,' she thought miserably. 'I just haven't got time to open the door and let Timmy out – I'll have to manage without him!'

At that very moment the truck started to move. With one last effort, George jumped up and grabbed the tailboard with both hands. Then she acrobatically hauled herself up into the back of the truck. They turned the corner of the road, accelerating. Once again, George was in the thick of an adventure – although this one didn't feel like being much fun!

Lying on the hard floor of the truck, the little girl had difficulty getting her breath back. She was feeling very cross with herself for stumbling over that crate, and then knocking the apples over. All that had delayed her – and most of all, she was sorry she hadn't got faithful old Timmy with her.

'I just didn't stop to think,' she told herself. 'Well, I'd better take a good look at the situation now!'

At least she could console herself by thinking she hadn't lost Chocabloc, because there he was, lying beside her! But what could she do against two strong men? How could she get the stolen statue away from them?

'Chocabloc's far too heavy for me to carry him off all by myself,' thought George unhappily. 'All I can do is let these men drive me to their hideout, and then go and tell the police!' What was more, she knew she must make sure she herself wasn't discovered.

After deciding on the best thing to do in the circumstances, George looked cautiously round her.

Nothing but a flap of tarpaulin separated the driver's cab from the back of the truck but unless they undid this flap and lifted it, the two men couldn't see they had an extra passenger. 'So that's *one* good thing,' George told herself hopefully.

Chocabloc was covered by another piece of tarpaulin. George thought it would be sensible to slip under this covering herself and let it hide her too. So she did. It was rather uncomfortable, but she felt safer now. Then she went on working things out.

'Now, what will happen when we get to the end of our journey?' she wondered. 'When the thieves come to get the statue, they'll find me as well! Oh, I know what! They'll have to get out of the driver's cab and come round to the back of the truck – so then I'll be able to move over into the front seats myself. At least, I *hope* I'll be able to! If not – well, I'll have to hope for the best!'

George saw, only too clearly, that she was in a tight spot. She tried to feel optimistic, all the same. If only she had had her cousins with her, or at least her beloved old Timmy!

The truck had been bumping noisily along a road full of ruts for some time now, and poor George was getting badly jolted. Suddenly, the jolting and the noise both died down a bit. Peering out of her hiding place, George saw that they were driving along a proper road now – in fact, it looked like the main road.

Suddenly she pricked up her ears. The two men were talking, and George could hear their voices well enough to be able to make out some of what they were saying.

'Well, how about that, Chuck? Everything's gone the way I planned it so far – you might congratulate me!'

George recognised the dark-haired man's slight sing-song accent.

'Yeah, okay!' said the driver, gruffly. 'But it might not have worked, you know! When I called the antique dealer from that public phone, making out I was the police, I reckoned he'd just shut up shop, put the Closed notice on the door, and be in such a state he'd forget to take the statue in, like you worked it out. I said the police wanted to see him urgently, so I guess he wouldn't have had the time. But it was real bad luck those kids were with him – and one of 'em stayed behind with the dog, to look after the place!'

'Never mind that now! You must admit I did pretty well, disposing of the kid and the dog so neatly. What are you complaining of?'

'I'm not complaining, Luis, just saying it could easily have failed, that's all. However, now we've got that great lump of wood the boss is so keen on, and . . .'

The truck lurched, and the man called Chuck swore. So far as George could tell, he'd nearly run over a turkey which was crossing the road because, all of a sudden, it didn't want to get to the other side! In a few moments, the two men went on with their conversation, but the only new thing George learned was the 'boss' Luis and Chuck worked for had a foreign-sounding sort of name. She thought it was 'Kopak'.

'Well, *that* conversation sheds a little light on things,' said George to herself. 'It looks as if this is an organised gang. Now, all we need to know is just *why* the boss, Kopak, wants Chocabloc so much! That part of it's still a mystery – *and* I don't know where we're going yet, either, so that's another. I suppose I'll soon find out!'

The truck had been on the move for about half an hour now. George had to keep perfectly still, and she was getting pins and needles. She was beginning to feel sleepy, too, under the stuffy tarpaulin, when Chuck suddenly spoke in such a loud voice that she came wide awake again.

'Am I ever hot! Hot and thirsty!'

'So am I,' said Luis. 'How about a drink?'

'Yeah – we could both use a nice cold beer. We'll stop at the next pub we come to. We can telephone Kopak from there, too, and tell him it went okay.'

The truck drove a little farther, and then Chuck braked. George huddled down under the tarpaulin as they stopped.

'I hope to goodness they don't decide to come round and take a look at Chocabloc!' she thought.

At that moment, she heard the two men jumping down from the cab. They *did* seem to be coming round to the back of the truck. George didn't hesitate for a moment. Soundlessly, she emerged from her hiding place slipped under the tarpaulin flap and into the driver's cab, and lay flat on the front seat. But so far as she could tell from the sound of the footsteps, which were moving away now, she had been wrong. Luis and Chuck wanted a cool drink more than a look at the statue they'd stolen!

Cautiously, George sat up. When her eyes were level with the window on her right, she could see the back view of the two thieves as they walked into a building. There were green trees outside the public house, and it looked cool and welcoming – they went straight in without turning to look back.

George let out a huge sigh of relief. Not only had Luis and Chuck missed finding her – she was alone with Chocabloc now! Come what may, she must take advantage of her stroke of luck.

But just *how* could she go off with the statue? She sat and wondered about it. That wasn't going to be an easy question to answer. She thought hard, staring at the public house beside the road, as her inventive brain ran over various possibilities.

— 5 —

A Dangerous Drive

'As a last resort, I could push Chocabloc out of the truck and then underneath it,' thought George. 'And then – well, one of two things will happen. Either the men will drive off without suspecting anything, or they'll notice that the statue's gone, and then – no, the fact is I only have half a chance of succeeding with *that* idea!'

Then she thought of something else. 'I could go into the public house and accuse Luis and Chuck of theft, in front of the landlord and everybody else who's there,' she told herself. 'The question is, would people believe me? I'm only a child, and I expect they'd pay more attention to a couple of grown-up men. No, that's not a very good idea either. I must think of a better one!'

Time was passing, and she still hadn't found a solution to her problem. Luis and Chuck might come back any minute – and then she'd have

wasted her precious chance to get the statue back
from them.

'Supposing I rouse the people in there,' she
thought, 'even if they *do* believe me, Luis and
Chuck will have had plenty of time to drive away
before I get to the end of my story – and they'll take
the Inca god with them.'

Then, suddenly, she interrupted herself. She said
out loud, but under her breath, 'Time to drive away
– and take the Inca god with them!'

Her eyes grew round with excitement, and began
to sparkle mischievously. 'Well, old chap,' she
added, as if she were talking to the statue still
lying in the back of the truck under its tarpaulin,
'suppose *we* drive away first? How about that?'

She got into the driver's seat, sat there and looked
around her. Yes, Chuck had left the ignition keys on
the dashboard! She made sure she knew the position
of all the controls.

'You see, I was looking for a way to rescue you,
Chocabloc, and I do believe I've found it!' she went
on out loud. 'I can't carry you, because you're too
heavy, but I *have* got a perfectly good means of
transport – this truck, and you're already in it!'

Yes, this was the way to get out of her difficulty! She could just drive the men's truck away
– snatching both the talking statue *and* their means
of catching up with it from under their very noses.

Of course George was far too young to have

a driving licence, and she couldn't really drive either. But five months earlier, Aunt Fanny had taken driving lessons, and George herself had been very interested. She wanted to learn to drive a car just as soon as she was old enough! She had got her mother to explain all the controls and show her how the accelerator and brake and clutch were used. She thought just holding the wheel and steering the truck couldn't be all that difficult!

'And I'll be very, very careful to go slowly and not try turning or anything complicated like that,' thought George. 'I'll just crawl along to the nearest village. I'm sure to find a police station there.'

Brave as George was, however, she did feel her hands trembling a little when she took hold of the wheel and turned the ignition key which the men had so luckily left in its place. But she managed to start the engine at her first attempt. That was encouraging.

Carefully, she reached out for the clutch with her left foot. It seemed a long way off! However, she pushed it down and put the car into first gear. That bit was easy enough, because there was a little diagram on the dashboard showing you which way to move the gear lever for the different gears. Then she slowly raised her left foot off the clutch while pushing down on the accelerator with her right foot, just as she had seen Aunt Fanny do.

Poor George! She suddenly found herself being

shaken about like a rattle! It was as if the truck had hiccups. But the ambitious young 'driver' clung to the wheel, gritted her teeth, and carried on. She was determined to escape with Chocabloc! She simply *had* to succeed. 'Hang on, old boy!' she told the Bolivian idol.

Setting her jaw grimly, she accelerated again, and the truck began to go a little faster. It wasn't hiccuping so much now. But poor George had great difficulty keeping it on the left-hand side of the road. It would wobble about so!

She hadn't gone more than a couple of hundred yards when she thought she heard a lot of noise and shouting behind her. Had Luis and Chuck started off in pursuit? The truck was still going forward, sometimes quite smoothly, sometimes in bumps and jerks, and George simply dared not look in the rear view mirror. She was intent on just keeping going.

Oh, help – there was a sharp bend in the road ahead of her! George clenched her teeth, grasped the wheel firmly, and went into the bend – but without braking at all, as she should have done.

A car was coming in the opposite direction, too. George thought she wasn't far enough over to the left – and she turned the steering wheel much too suddenly. She swerved off course, and had an impression of a tree rushing to meet her. She tried to turn the wheel the other way, but it was too late! Her foot reached for the brake pedal, but she had no time to touch it. The truck was going to hit that tree head on.

At the time George didn't know how on earth she'd managed to escape unharmed! It was explained to her later that since the road went uphill round the bend, the truck, which was going very slowly anyway, had slowed down even more at the moment of the accident. So, very fortunately, the only damage done was to the bonnet of the truck where it hit the tree.

Whatever had happened, anyway, George realised that she was safe and sound – though suddenly and unexpectely sitting on a grassy bank! The impact had thrown Chocabloc out of the back of the truck, too. So there they both were, safe on the grass by the roadside.

George was badly shaken, but she got up and looked round. Three farm workers were already running up from the far end of a field nearby. The car which had been travelling in the opposite direction had stopped. A man, a woman and a little girl got out and ran over to George.

'Are you hurt?' asked the man. 'Where are the others?'

'I *think* I'm all right,' said George, feeling herself all over. 'And there aren't any others – I was on my own.'

One of the farm workers frowned. 'Don't you try to be funny with us, young man!' he told George.

'Lads of your age aren't allowed to drive! Joy-riding in your Dad's truck, eh? You'd better own up!'

'More likely he pinched the truck, if you ask me,' said one of the other men.

George usually rather liked being taken for a boy – but she couldn't stand the idea of being taken for a *thief*! She prided herself on being absolutely frank and honest. Red in the face, she drew herself up proudly. 'I haven't pinched anything!' she said indignantly. 'In fact, I was trying to get away from some thieves when I had this accident!'

'Oh, so the thieves were running after you?' said the driver of the car, rather sarcastically. 'Things are usually the other way round!'

'It certainly doesn't sound a very likely story,' agreed his wife.

'Ooh, look!' cried the little girl. 'A big wooden dolly!' She pointed to Chocabloc lying in the grass.

'That's an Inca statue – the thieves had stolen it!' George explained.

'And that's how it came to be in your truck?' asked the first farm worker who had spoken. He obviously didn't believe a word she said! 'That's enough tall stories, my lad – it's off to the police station for *you*!'

George wished to goodness she could get them to believe her. She was afraid that if they took her off to a police station, Chocabloc would just be left lying by the roadside, where Luis and Chuck could easily pick him up.

'I'll be more than happy to go to the police with you,' she said. 'I was going there of my own accord anyway! But someone must guard this statue while we're gone.'

The little girl jumped up and down excitedly. 'Me! Me! I want to look after the dolly!' she cried.

'Hush, Valerie!' said her mother. 'You're just being silly, dear!'

'All the same, that gives me an idea,' said the little girl's father. 'We'll take this lad to the police ourselves – he can come in the car with us, and as for the totem pole or whatever it is,' he added, turning to the farm workers, 'could you help me get it up on my roof rack?'

They soon had Chocabloc on the roof of the car. George was feeling much happier now! Of course, she was worried about the damage to the truck, because she knew that had been her fault – she didn't mind so much if it belonged to Luis or Chuck, but she suspected they had stolen it, and she knew very well she ought not to have been trying to drive it. But at the same time, she was glad to think she'd outwitted the thieves. In a few moments, she and the Inca god would be safe at a police station.

Obediently, she got into the car beside the driver. His name turned out to be Mr Lawrence. Little Valerie and her mother got into the back seat, and

the car started off. Mr Lawrence had told the farm
workers, who were witnesses to the accident, that he
was going to the police station in the nearest village
– it was called Sandborne St James. George realised
they would be passing the public house where Luis
and Chuck had stopped. And sure enough, just as
they were approaching the place, she saw the two
men by the side of the road! They must have been
trying to hitch a lift, because they were about to
climb into a car that had stopped for them.

'Oh, please stop, sir!' she cried. 'Stop! Those are
the two thieves! There they are, beside that car!
Don't let them get away.'

'You don't cut any ice with me, my boy!' said Mr
Lawrence, in an unfriendly voice. 'I suppose you
think that if we stop you'll be able to slip away from
me, but you won't do that! I've got you safe, and
I'm not letting you go!'

As for Luis and Chuck, they had seen George
– *and* they had spotted the talking statue on the
roof of the Lawrences' car, too! Realising that they
couldn't hope to get the idol back now, they quickly
clambered into the car that had offered them a lift,
and it drove on again – going the opposite way from
Mr Lawrence, of course. At this point, the two men
were only too thankful to get away, even without
the statue!

George was frantic. 'Mr Lawrence, I'm not lying!'
she said. 'Please, *please* turn round! We must follow

those gangsters to their hideout, and then we'll know where to find their leader.'

Little Valerie was listening to George with her mouth wide open. How exciting all this was – as good as going to the pictures! But her father just smiled.

'You certainly have a vivid imagination,' he told George. 'Well, I'm sure your story is very entertaining – and all you have to do is tell it to the police and hope *they* believe you! Here we are, by the look of it!'

The car stopped outside Sandborne St James police station. It was painted white and had some tubs of flowers outside, so it looked rather welcoming – but the sergeant on duty inside gave the Lawrences and George a chilly reception. However, once he realised there had been an accident, he told Mr Lawrence, 'Carry on, then. I'm listening.'

Mr Lawrence immediately plunged into his own version of what had happened. 'This young lad was all alone at the wheel of the truck. It's a miracle it didn't crash into our own car head-on – we were coming the opposite way. If you ask me, either it belongs to his father and he was joy-riding, or he'd stolen it – perhaps he'd also stolen the curious statue we found in the grass beside him. You can see it out there, on top of my car.'

The sergeant glanced at the driving licence Mr Lawrence showed him to prove his identity, and then turned to George. 'Right, lad, what's *your* story?' he said, looking very stern. 'You can tell us who you are, for a start – and if you try lying it'll be the worse for you!'

'I *never* tell lies!' protested George! 'And I say everything Mr Lawrence has just told you, or nearly everything, is quite wrong!'

'What? How dare you! Are you accusing *me* of lying?' shouted Valerie's father. 'You'd better be careful what you say, my boy!'

'And I'm not even a boy, either, so there!' said George indignantly. 'My name's Georgina Kirrin, and my father is Quentin Kirrin, the famous scientist – he's very well known round here! What's more, I really didn't steal that truck! Well . . . well, not in the first place, and when I did take it, it wasn't actually *stealing*. You see, it was carrying a valuable wooden statue stolen from an antique dealer by the two men who were driving it. I'd managed to get in the truck too, and when they stopped to have something to drink, I seized my chance and took the wheel – and started the engine. I was going to drive to the nearest police station and get the two thieves arrested, but – well, my plan went a bit wrong, and I'm . . . well, I *am* sorry about that part of it!'

Even the police sergeant couldn't help noticing the obvious honesty in George's face and voice, and by now Mr and Mrs Lawrence were looking at her with surprise and interest. Little Valerie clapped her hands and laughed with glee. 'Ooh, you're a girl!' she cried. 'You're a girl!'

The sergeant certainly did know Uncle Quentin's name, and he asked George some more questions about her adventure. She was more than happy to give him a detailed account of all that had happened.

'All right,' said the sergeant at last. He believed her now! 'We'll telephone your father, Miss Kirrin.'

George felt a bit scared. She knew how strict her father was, and felt sure he'd punish her for what she had done that afternoon.

'Oh, please,' she asked the sergeant, 'could you telephone Mr Barry Lane and the Kirrin antique shop too? You see, the Bolivian god really belongs to him, and he'll be so glad to get it back!'

So the sergeant rang both numbers. When Uncle Quentin answered, he didn't spend much time talking. 'I'm on my way!' he said curtly, and that was all.

Barry Lane was more talkative, and said he'd come as fast as he possibly could, bringing Julian, Dick and Anne with him – and Timmy too, of course!

The sergeant told two constables to take Chocabloc off the roof rack, and while they were doing that, George impatiently waited for her cousins. She just hoped they'd be the first to arrive!

Uncle Quentin is Cross

For once that day, George was in luck! Barry and her cousins *did* arrive at the police station before Uncle Quentin. As soon as the station wagon stopped in Sandborne St James, Timmy jumped out and rushed into the building. He flung himself at George and licked her face lovingly all over with his big wet tongue.

'Woof! Woof!' he barked.

'Oh, darling Timmy – how I've missed you!' cried George.

Timmy had been so carried away by his enthusiasm that he'd almost knocked little Valerie over as he passed her! Mrs Lawrence leaned forward to catch the little girl, lost her own balance and knocked into her husband – and Mr Lawrence lost *his* balance and staggered against the sergeant's desk. The sergeant put out a hand to help him, and accidentally swept a whole pile of papers off the desk. They flew about all over the place! George and the Lawrence family bent down to pick up the papers, and so did the sergeant and two constables. Timmy went on leaping about and barking. What a noise there was! Then Barry, Julian, Dick and Anne followed Timmy into the room, and soon everyone was down on the floor on all fours. Timmy was very happy – he thought they'd all gone down on the floor so as to be on his own level, and he affectionately licked everything he came across, arms, hands, faces, and even the sergeant's moustache.

At last the three policemen got up, rather red in the face. The papers were all back on the desk now, and gradually everybody calmed down. At last you could hear yourself speak! Barry, Julian, Dick and Anne clustered around George.

'We were worried to death when we found the shop closed and Timmy shut inside it!'

'We just couldn't think what had become of you, George!'

'And then we saw Chocabloc had gone, too!'

'So we realised he must have been stolen, and we guessed you'd be chasing the thieves!'

They were all talking at once – and the Lawrences were listening, and looking rather stunned! The sergeant banged on the table to get them to be quiet. Then, turning to Barry, he said, 'Now, let's hear *your* story, sir! Do I understand that the statue my men were unloading just now is your property, and was stolen from you?'

So Barry told his own story. 'I expect you can guess what had happened! That telephone call was simply a trick to get me away from my shop. And I was idiot enough to go dashing straight off to Kirrin police station!'

The antique dealer went on to explain that when he got there, the policemen had been very surprised to see him. They'd assured him that they had never telephoned to ask him to come along, and no one suspected him of hit-and-run driving.

'So then I knew someone had been tricking me. I hurried back to my shop, with the children here, but it was too late! George and the Inca god had gone. And but for George herself, I'd have lost a valuable antique. She really is an excellent detective – brave, fearless, clever – '

'And also *extremely* disobedient!' said a very stern voice.

Everyone turned round. There was Uncle Quentin, standing in the doorway. He had come into the police station unnoticed, and had been listening to Barry's story. Obviously, *he* didn't feel like singing George's praises! He was annoyed at being dragged away from his important work, too, and he looked at his daughter with a cross expression on his face. George bravely stood her ground and looked him in the eye.

'I just hadn't got time to ring you up and tell you what was happening, Father,' she explained. 'I mean, there was a crime being committed before my very eyes! What would *you* have done in my place? Wouldn't you have chased the thief yourself?'

'That's not the point!' said Uncle Quentin, clicking his tongue angrily. 'You must have known how dangerous it was to go after those men, especially all on your own! Once and for all, Georgina, you must cure yourself of your ridiculous rashness!'

'But, Father – '

'And no buts about it! You will be severely punished.'

The sound of the telephone ringing interrupted him. The sergeant picked up the receiver, and after a few minutes' conversation with whoever was at the other end of the line, he hung up again and looked at Uncle Quentin.

'Well, I've got some more news now,' he said. 'Your daughter has told us the number of the gangsters' truck, which she sensibly noted down before coming here with Mr and Mrs Lawrence, and just as she thought, it *was* a stolen vehicle. As for the men themselves, we've circulated a description of them, but so far there's been no trace of them. I suppose they've gone to ground.' He smiled, looking much less fierce than before, and added, 'If I were you, sir, I wouldn't be too hard on Miss Kirrin here! She's full of pluck and initiative! But for her, Mr Lane would have lost a valuable piece of property.'

'I know how to deal with my own daughter, thank you very much!' snapped Uncle Quentin.

The sergeant opened his mouth to say something else, and then thought better of it. George kept quiet, too. Uncle Quentin sounded so crushing that Barry didn't like to speak up for his young friend again, and as for Julian, Dick and Anne, they were feeling very sorry for George, but they knew it would be better not to argue with their uncle – or at least, not now. Perhaps he wouldn't be so cross later on.

Soon all the statements had been signed, and once these formalities were over Uncle Quentin, Barry Lane and the Five found themselves outside Sandborne St James police station again. The two constables had kindly put Chocabloc into Barry's station wagon. The antique dealer went over to George's father. There was a rather worried look on Barry's pleasant face.

'Sir,' he said, sounding rather awkward, 'I already owe your daughter a great deal – but I'm wondering if I could ask *you* a favour too? I really would be very grateful if you'd help me.'

'What is it?' asked Uncle Quentin.

'Well – if it's not too much trouble, could you keep this wooden statue at your own house for a while? If I take it back to the shop, I'm afraid those crooks may come back and try to steal it again. But if it was at Kirrin Cottage they'd never know where to find it.'

Uncle Quentin smiled. 'Why, yes – of course I'll keep it safe for you!' he said. 'Just follow my car to Kirrin Cottage – and you children jump in!'

So the car set off, followed by Barry's station wagon. When they reached Kirrin Cottage, the two men put Chocabloc in the garden shed. Aunt Fanny was delighted to see the children home safe and sound.

'I was so worried when I heard you'd gone rushing off into danger yet again!' she told George. 'Oh dear, George – will you *ever* learn not to go meddling in such things, darling?'

'Mother, there simply wasn't anything else I could do!' said George.

Anne felt she must speak up for her cousin. 'Aunt Fanny,' she begged, 'when Uncle Quentin comes in, couldn't you put in a good word for George? He said he was going to punish her severely.'

'And she really doesn't deserve it,' added Dick.

'Yes – *would* you try and get a more lenient sentence?' asked Julian too.

'Well, children, I promise you I'll try!' Aunt Fanny told them.

But there was no getting round Uncle Quentin this time! 'As you know, we were all going to the cinema tomorrow evening,' he told his daughter. 'Well, now I shall take your mother and your cousins, but you will have to stay behind.'

The film being shown at the local cinema was an exciting adventure, and George had particularly wanted to see it. Feeling very sad, she bit her lip, but said nothing. Kind little Anne's eyes filled with tears, and she tried to make her uncle change his mind, but he stopped her as soon as she began speaking.

'There's no point in going on about it, Anne! George must learn not to be so foolhardy – it's in her own best interests.'

Then Uncle Quentin changed the subject, and told them that Barry Lane said he had definitely decided not to sell the Inca statue until he was back in London. However, as it had caused so much trouble, he thought it would be safer not to display it in Kirrin any more.

The children were still puzzled by the mystery of Chocabloc. *Why* were Luis and Chuck – or rather, their mysterious boss Kopak – so keen to have the statue that they would pay any price to get it? For Barry had said that although it was a valuable antique, it wasn't worth all the money they had offered him before they tried to steal the idol. The question was still occupying them when they went to bed.

'I'm so sorry you can't come to the cinema with

us tomorrow, George!' said Anne, before the girls put the light out in their room.

'Oh, who cares?' said George, as if she didn't mind. 'I can always have my own adventures – I don't need to watch adventures on a film! And we're going to come out on top in *this* adventure, as usual. You just wait and see! The Famous Five *always* come out on top!' And she switched off the light.

Next day the weather was rather wet, and the children were in a gloomy mood. They tried going out, but they'd soon had enough of the drizzle which didn't look as if it was ever going to stop. They spent the afternoon playing board games indoors. Julian, Dick and Anne weren't particularly looking forward to going to the cinema without George, even though they had all wanted to see the film in the first place. As for George, she pretended to be very cheerful, but she was only putting on an act.

That evening, when her parents and her cousins had left the house, she was glad she could stop pretending! There was no one there but herself, Timmy, and old Joan, who sometimes came up from the village to help Aunt Fanny in the house, and who had offered to stay late today and cook George's supper. *She* felt sorry for the little girl too, and fried her a specially delicious plateful of eggs, sausages and bacon to try and make up for the treat she was missing, but somehow George didn't feel very hungry, and it wasn't much fun eating a meal without the others there to talk to. After her supper, she helped Joan wash up, and then went out into the garden to play with Timmy.

'I suppose I'm lucky, really!' she told her faithful dog. 'If Father had said I couldn't have *you* with me, it would have been a much worse punishment! We're never really bored when we're together, are we, Timmy?'

'Woof!' agreed Timmy, jumping up at her. 'Woof!'

But soon it began to get dark, and they went back indoors. Joan had finished tidying up the kitchen. 'Well, I'll be getting along home,' she told George. 'Are you sure you'll be all right on your own, Miss Georgina?'

'Yes, of course I will!' George assured her, and Joan said good night.

After a while, in spite of her brave words to Timmy, George realised that she *did* feel bored. 'Oh, what shall we do to pass the time, Timmy dear?' she asked, sighing. 'Wait a minute – I know! Why don't we go and visit Chocabloc in the garden shed? If there *is* some mystery about him that we haven't found yet, now or never is my chance to discover it! I've got him all to myself, with plenty of time to investigate. So come on, Timmy!'

George knew there was only a rather weak electric light bulb in the shed, so she thought it would be a good idea to take her torch, which had a brand new battery in it. She was going to examine the Inca god inch by inch if she had to! Suppose there was a secret compartment in the wood he was made of? It might contain an important message, or a map showing buried treasure, or the formula for some amazing invention dating back to the time of the Incas themselves!

Followed by Timmy, George left the house and made for the shed. The garden was bathed in moonlight. George had got the key of the shed out of her father's desk, and she put it into the lock and turned it. The door opened with a faint squeal of its hinges.

George let Timmy in first, and then followed him and closed the door after her. Chocabloc looked stranger and more impressive than ever in the dim light of the bulb dangling from the roof.

'*You* don't give away your secrets in a hurry, do you, old chap?' muttered George, switching on her torch. She shone its bright beam on the wooden statue. 'Now, where shall I begin?'

At that moment Timmy, standing beside her, growled softly and made for the door. Something – or someone – had attracted his attention.

— 7 —

The Secret of the Inca God

George had very good reactions, and she moved swiftly. 'Ssh!' she told the dog, going to the door herself. She switched off the light bulb and her own torch. Then she stood there motionless in the dark, with one hand on Timmy's back, straining her ears. She felt the dog's coat bristling beneath her fingers. 'Ssh!' she repeated, warning him.

Then she heard voices.

'That fool of an antique dealer – he thought he'd hoodwinked us!'

'Yeah, that's where they put the statue, sure enough!'

'And I saw the whole family leave in their car.'

'Okay, then – my skeleton keys will soon pick this lock.'

Luis and Chuck! They had walked round the shed to the door. Its walls were only made of thin wood, so that sounds outside could be heard quite easily, but in any case the two men weren't even taking the trouble to lower their voices. They obviously thought Kirrin Cottage was completely empty.

'They must have followed us all at a distance yesterday,' thought George, 'and seen my father and Barry put the statue in here. They certainly know where to look for it!'

She was in a tight spot. She'd thwarted the two men's plans once already – and if they found her here, they would probably want their revenge on her for that! Afterwards, they'd go off with Chocabloc, and she would be powerless to prevent them.

Well, there was no time to feel frightened! George knew she had to do something, so she thought fast.

'This gang evidently won't stop at anything to get hold of Chocabloc,' she told herself. 'So somehow I must make sure he doesn't fall into their hands. But *how*? I'm alone here with Timmy, and old Chocabloc doesn't look as if he could defend himself, let alone me too!'

Then, suddenly, a gleam came into George's eyes. Her train of thought had just given her an idea! Chocabloc *had* got one way of defending himself – and her. A very good way, too!

Without wasting any time, George put her plan into action. Very stealthily, she crept over to stand behind the statue. Timmy trotted after her. Thinking the door was locked, one of the men was already getting to work on the lock with a skeleton key.

George stood on tiptoe and called through the mask-like face of the statue.

'Who's that? I heard a noise at the door – do you hear that, Father?'

Then she shouted, at the top of her voice, 'You're right! I'll go and see!' Amplified by the mask, the noise she made was like thunder.

There was not a sound from the two men on the other side of the door. George guessed they must be standing rooted to the spot with terror! The statue acted as a sound-box, distorting and amplifying her voice so that it echoed round the shed and sounded like several people talking. Chuck and Luis must be thinking there were at least two fierce, determined, loud-voiced men in here!

'I'll just let the dogs loose before I open the door!' George added, shouting through the mouth of the statue again.

She emerged from the hollow back of the statue, picked up Timmy, and held him level with Chocabloc's face, inside the mask. 'Woof, Timmy! Go on, good dog – bark!' she told him.

Timmy got the idea, and happily started barking as loud as he could. 'Woof! *Woof*! WOOF!'

Holding him at arm's length, George moved him back from the mask and then close to it again. There was really only one dog barking, but he sounded like a whole pack of hounds.

Quick footsteps scurrying away outside told George

that her clever idea had worked. She put Timmy down and began laughing to herself. The gangsters had taken to their heels! She didn't think they'd be back in a hurry.

However, George decided to postpone her investigation of the statue – she didn't want to risk being taken by surprise, and she thought it would be better if she simply guarded it until the family came home. So she patrolled the garden for nearly two hours, with the faithful Timmy beside her. But nothing else happened.

Aunt Fanny and Uncle Quentin were rather surprised to find George still up when they came home from the cinema, but they thought she had already been punished enough, so they didn't scold her. And she didn't mention the attempted theft of the statue to them – but as her cousins got out of the car she whispered, 'I say – while you were all out, Chuck and Luis came back. They were trying to steal Chocabloc again! But Timmy and I soon dealt with them!'

'George, what happened?' asked Julian, alarmed. 'Quick, tell us!'

'Let's go up to the attic,' said George. 'We can talk there!'

So a few moments later, the Five had said good night to Uncle Quentin and Aunt Fanny, and were holding a council of war among all the old trunks and cardboard cartons stored up in the attic. George's cousins were eager to hear her story. 'Oh, you must have been so frightened!' said Anne.

'Don't be an ass, Anne!' said Dick. 'George is never frightened!'

'Well – I was *nearly* frightened!' George admitted. And she told them all about her adventure. 'This time,' she finished, 'I don't think we want to tell my father or even Barry what happened – my father would be angry, and Barry would only worry. I suggest we say nothing about it at the moment. We'll make our own inquiries into the case!'

'As usual!' said Julian, smiling. He knew how independent his cousin was! 'One thing I can do, though, is fit an extra lock to the door of that shed. I saw a new lock in Uncle Quentin's toolbox.'

'I do wonder why they're so set on stealing Chocabloc!' said Anne. 'I mean, it's not as if he were made of solid gold or anything!'

'Or even a specially rare type of wood, according to Barry,' added Dick.

'Yes – and it wouldn't be easy for art thieves to disguise him if they wanted to sell him again,' said Julian thoughtfully. 'Who would want him? Some rich collector who likes old wooden idols, perhaps?'

'I'm more and more certain that there's yet another secret to the talking statue,' said George. 'Actually, I was just going to take a really thorough look at him again when Luis and Chuck turned up.'

'Well, why don't we go and do that now – all of us?' said Dick, jumping up.

'Yes, why not?' agreed George. 'Come on, everyone! My parents have gone to bed, so we must be careful not to make any noise.'

Going in single file, the Five tiptoed downstairs – or in Timmy's case, tip-pawed! They reached the shed easily enough, and crept silently inside.

George gave Anne her torch. 'You shine its light on the statue, Anne, while we have a really good look,' she told the little girl. 'Julian and Dick, could you pick Chocabloc up and put him down flat on the floor? That'll make it easier for us to examine him.'

The two boys took hold of the statue. They were handling it very gently, but just as they were going to put it down flat, Timmy, who was chasing an imaginary mouse, ran between Dick's legs and made him stumble. He let go of the Inca god's head, and the head and torso hit the floor with a loud thump.

'Oh, my goodness!' said George, horrified. 'I only hope we haven't damaged poor Chocabloc. Barry wouldn't be very pleased!'

Julian bent down to see if the statue was all right, while Anne shone the torch on it. 'Oh, help!' he said, in dismay. 'You've done it now, Dick! Just look at that!'

George, Dick and Anne leaned forward. Julian

was pointing at the statue's chest, which was deco-
rated with a sort of breastplate design carved in the
wood. It was shaped like a sun – and the shock of
the fall seemed to have cracked the carving.

'Bother, bother, *bother*!' said Dick unhappily.
'Barry will be furious, and I don't blame him.
Hand me the torch, Anne, so I can see just how
much damage I've done.'

He shone the beam right on the crack in the wood
– and saw something gleaming inside.

'Why – this breastplate is hollow!' he cried. 'And
there's something underneath – something shiny.
Hang on a sec, while I try to get it out with
my knife!'

He quickly snapped open the big blade of his
new penknife and bent over the wooden breastplate.
Now the children could see that the sun-shaped
design was really like the lid of a box – but it fitted
the statue so well that it looked as if it was all carved
out of the same piece of solid wood. Of course, the
idol had already been given a jolt when it fell out of
the gansters' truck, and this final bump had shifted
the breastplate out of position and away from the
rest of the statue. Feeling very excited. Dick slipped
the blade of his knife into the crack. First it touched
something soft, then something hard.

'Wait a minute!' said Julian. 'I'm sure there's a
long, thin pair of pincers in Uncle Quentin's toolbox
– I'll get them.'

The pincers did the trick. The others watched, fascinated, as Dick pulled a large wad of cotton wool out from under the wooden breastplate.

'But that can't be what we saw shining just now,' said Anne.

'No,' agreed George. 'I expect the cotton wool was just padding put round something else to protect it. Try again, Dick!'

Dick probed about inside the crack with the pincers one more, and this time he brought up a sparkling stone – or almost brought it up, but it was obviously fixed to something larger, because although he could get it level with the crack in the carving he couldn't get it out. He let the stone go, and it slipped back out of sight.

'We'll have to get the breastplate right off the statue,' said Julian. 'Then we'll be able to take a better look.'

He found a chisel which he could use as a lever, and that did the trick. The sun-shaped wooden breastplate came off the statue, just like a box lid. And inside, packed round with cotton wool, there was an amazing piece of jewellery – an exact copy of the wooden breastplate that had been covering it, but made of shining gold and set with precious stones!

The children held their breath as they looked at their wonderful find. Even Timmy seemed fascinated. The 'sun' consisted of a golden disc with rays round the edges, and the rays ended in huge transparent and green stones. The children didn't know a lot about jewels, but it was easy to guess that they were priceless diamonds and emeralds. So *this* was the real secret of the talking statue's value!

'Well – Chocabloc's come clean about himself at last!' said George.

'What a treasure chest!' breathed Julian. 'Worn *on* his chest, too!'

'That explains why the man called Kopak was so keen to get hold of him,' said Dick. 'The wooden statue must have been just a way to get these precious stones into the country illegally! But where does Barry fit into all this, I wonder?'

'I'm sure *he* can't be one of the gang,' said Anne, 'so why was the statue sent to him in the first place?'

The three older children looked at each other. Quiet little Anne had pointed out a very important part of the puzzle.

'You're right, it *is* odd!' said George. 'Well, here's another mystery! If Barry were in the plot, surely he'd have removed the golden disc from its hiding place ages ago, so he can't know anything about it!'

'The others do, though,' said Julian. 'If you ask me, Chocabloc was sent to Barry by mistake. We must try to find out just what happened. I wonder if Barry's still got the crate and wrappings the statue came in.'

'I bet he hasn't!' said Dick. 'You know Barry –
he's very bad at keeping track of papers, and anyway
he told us he always throws away the packaging
materials his antiques arrive in at once, so he hasn't
got them cluttering the place up. If Chocabloc *was*
sent to the wrong address, I shouldn't think we'll
ever find out the right one now.'

'Then what can we do?' asked Anne.

'Pursue our inquiries and try to catch the gangsters!' said George, with determination.

Julian looked at his cousin, frowning slightly.
'George, hadn't we better go and tell the police?'
he said.

'No, Ju, certainly not! Listen – if we tell the police
our story, the newspapers are bound to get hold of it
too. And Kopak, Luis and Chuck, not to mention
any other members of the gang we may not know
about yet, will hear that the police are on their track
and clear out in a hurry – leaving us with precious
little hope they'll ever be brought to justice!'

'It *would* be a pity to let them get away,' said
Dick. 'What do you bet they're part of a huge
international organisation? They're probably out to
cheat the Customs all over the world, importing
precious works of art illegally. George is right –
let's keep this to ourselves a bit longer.'

'Dick, honestly, you must know the police are
really the people to deal with this sort of crime!'
Julian insisted. 'Not us!'

'Oh, Ju, please listen!' George interrupted pleadingly. 'I've got such a good plan! We can set a trap here, in this very shed. When you think how much is at stake for the gang, they're sure to have another go at stealing Chocabloc. Wouldn't it be wonderful to catch them in the act?'

George explained her plan to her cousins, and Julian had to admit that it *was* a good one. He agreed to do as George wanted and keep what they knew to themselves for a little longer. Then they set to work at once to carry out the plan. Dick carefully fitted the wooden breastplate back into position, and Julian, who was good with his hands, made a clever electrical device and linked it to a big alarm clock fixed inside the head of the statue. It would ring a loud bell if anyone tried to pick Chocabloc up – and the mask of the idol's face would amplify the sound of the bell, so that they could hardly help being woken up in Kirrin Cottage.

'Now we must just wait for the alarm to go off – and I'm sure it *will*, one night soon,' said George. 'We must all be ready to rush out at a moment's notice!'

When the children went indoors to bed at last, George was carrying the beautiful golden breastplate. She planned to hand it over to Barry Lane next day.

In the morning, Barry was astonished to hear the story the children had to tell him as they and Timmy sat drinking tea with him in the back room of his shop. Barry had come to know their tastes now, and he had a bottle of orange squash for anyone who didn't feel like tea!

'And to convince you every word of it is true – just take a look at this!' said George dramatically at the end of her tale. And she produced the huge, beautiful piece of jewellery from the old box she had brought it in.

At the sight of the golden breastplate, the antique dealer simply stared! His mouth dropped open. 'But . . . but this . . . my goodness!' he stammered. 'Good God – good *Inca* god! I've never seen anything like it in my life!'

He sounded so comical the four children had to laugh, and Timmy joined in, barking enthusiastically. But by now Barry was examining the jewels and their golden setting through a magnifying glass.

'Amazing workmanship!' he was murmuring. 'It's obviously very old – there's no doubt that it's genuine. Wonderful stones! This is a real museum piece!' He still looked as if he could hardly believe his eyes. 'I must put this breastplate in a bank vault in the nearest town,' he added. 'But though I see what you mean about not scaring the gangsters away, George, I think perhaps we ought to go to the police and tell them about your find!'

'Oh, Barry, please don't!' said Dick. 'Not yet! I

agree with George – it would be maddening if the crooks disappeared now, and if they find out the police are after them that's what they *will* do, and then we'll never catch them and their boss!'

Barry himself had a certain liking for adventure – so in the end he let the children have their own way!

'I think the best way to start our investigation is by looking hard at any *other* antiques you had delivered at the same time as the talking statue,' said Julian.

'And the packaging of the statue itself, if you've still got it,' Anne remembered.

'I'm afraid I must have thrown all that away by now,' said Barry. 'But as it happens, the other items from that delivery are still in the shop. I haven't sold any of them yet.'

It turned out that the 'other items' were all small bronze urns. A whole consignment of them had been delivered from Bolivia, along with Chocabloc. The children and the antique dealer looked at them very carefully, but there didn't seem to be anything at all odd about them.

'The one thing I *am* sure of,' said Barry, 'is that I never ordered the statue or these urns myself. And I finally got round to writing to my partner Alan the other day, and I had a reply this morning. He says he didn't order anything from Bolivia either.'

'So I was right,' said George triumphantly. 'These things were addressed to you by mistake! Oh, if only we could find out who they were really meant for!'

However, it was far too late for that. Without any of the packaging, which must have been labelled, there was no hope of finding out either the address to which the Bolivian antiques *should* have been delivered, or the sender's address, or anything else which might give a useful clue.

'Oh well, no use crying over spilt milk!' said Julian. 'We must just be on the alert and wait for the gang to make the next move!'

'And perhaps something else will happen to help us, if we're lucky,' said Anne.

'I don't believe in luck!' said Dick. 'I'd rather trust in the working of our fine alarm system!'

But as it was to turn out, Dick was wrong there!

8

On the Inca Trail

Three days and three nights went by, and the gang still hadn't shown any more interest in Chocabloc. Nothing much happened at all, in fact, except that Aunt Fanny and Uncle Quentin went away for a week's holiday on their own. They had been planning to do that for a long time – it was a pity that the only time Uncle Quentin could manage to leave his work was during the school holidays, Aunt Fanny said, but she had arranged for kind old Joan to come and sleep at the house, cook the children meals, and look after them.

George found it very frustrating, waiting for something to happen. She kept waking up in the night with a start, thinking she heard the alarm bell in the shed ringing – but it never did ring.

One morning, however, the children heard a very interesting news item on the radio. They were out in the garden doing some weeding, as a nice surprise for Uncle Quentin when he got home. They had brought the transistor radio out of the house to amuse them while they worked, and soon there was a news bulletin. The newsreader read out several other headlines, and then said, 'It is reported from Peru and Bolivia that highly organised gangs who specialise in the looting of museums are active in those countries. The La Paz, Cuzco and Lima museums have already been burgled in this way. It is thought that the stolen curios and antiques, most of them dating from the Inca period, are being illegally exported to the United States and Europe, for private sale to rich art lovers.'

Then the newsreader went on to other subjects. Dick hurried over to the radio and twiddled its knobs, looking for another station broadcasting news. 'Did you hear that?' he asked excitedly. 'I say – I wonder if those thefts have anything to do with – ' But then he stopped short. He had found a radio station broadcasting a more detailed news bulletin.

'. . . Despite all efforts of the Bolivian police, the La Paz museum has still failed to recover the famous "Inca Sun" stolen over a month ago. This unique piece of jewellery, a solid gold disc representing the sun and surrounded by rays tipped with diamonds and emeralds, is considered almost priceless. Interpol has been alerted, but so far no trace of the Inca Sun has been found.'

Dick switched the radio off, and the children looked at each other in awe and amazement.

'Well!' breathed Julian. 'So now we know!'

Dropping their garden forks and trowels, the children got on their bicycles and raced off down the road to Kirrin village, with Timmy after them. But when they got to Barry Lane's antique shop they found it was crammed with a coachload of tourists on an outing who had stopped in Kirrin. So they just had to kill time as best they could while they waited for a chance to talk to him in private.

Julian was strolling past the Kirrin newsagent's when the cover of an art magazine in the window attracted his attention. Apparently this issue was all about the jewellery of the ancient Incas. What a coincidence! He went in and bought the magazine, and found it wasn't a coincidence at all – the articles had been written because of all the thefts of Inca treasures going on in South America. Among other items mentioned, the magazine described the famous Inca Sun that had been stolen in La Paz. However, the art expert writing about it knew much more than the radio newsreaders, and could give his readers extra details. Julian showed his magazine to the other children. They learnt that the gold disc was not actually solid after all, but a hollow case enclosing a wonderful opal disc engraved with magical inscriptions by the Inca priests. This 'Opal Sun' made the entire jewel doubly valuable.

As soon as Barry was free, they told him their news. He was more alarmed than delighted! 'Well, all we need now is for the police to discover that the Inca Sun's in the bank vault!' he sighed. 'Then they'll deduce that I'm acting as a receiver of stolen goods for the jewel thieves!'

'No, they won't, Barry!' George assured him. 'We can tell them you're not!'

'All the same, children, I do think that at this point we ought to go to the authorities. Now we know about the Opal Sun too, it really doesn't make sense to keep quiet any longer. Besides, the museum in La Paz will want its property back!'

'Yes, and *we* want to catch the thieves!' George reminded him. 'You don't want them to get off scot free, do you?'

She had some trouble persuading Barry to keep quiet a little longer, but for once she had the support of Julian, whose own blood was up now that he'd read the interesting magazine article. At last, rather reluctantly, Barry gave in to them.

However, as the children cycled back to Kirrin Cottage, George's mood changed. They weren't getting anywhere much after all, even if they knew a lot more about the Inca Sun than before! But nothing was happening – it was really maddening.

Kind little Anne saw that her cousin was in a bad temper, and tried to cheer her up. 'I expect the thieves will soon find out that Aunt Fanny and Uncle Quentin have gone away,' she reminded George, 'and they'll decide that makes it a good moment to come and kidnap Chocabloc. I'm sure they'll come back one night soon, and our alarm will go off, and – '

'And they may well get away after all!' George snapped crossly.

In fact, what happened at Kirrin Cottage that very night proved *both* girls partly right! The thieves did come back for Chocabloc – and they got away with him, too, because the alarm never went off.

The first hint the Five had of it was when they came down to breakfast in the morning and found old Joan in rather a bad temper.

'Which of you children left the garden gate open last night?' she asked. 'Haven't I told you over and over again to make sure it's locked after dark?'

George looked at Joan in surprise. 'Why, we none of us went out yesterday evening!' she said. 'We all stayed at home watching a television progamme.'

'Oh, then I suppose it was Timmy who unlocked the gate!' said Joan sarcastically. 'Because it was wide open this morning – anyone could have got in.'

The children looked at each other in alarm. The same thought had occurred to all of them. Chocabloc! Suppose the gangsters *had* got in – and had got away with him, too?

All together, they turned and ran to the shed.

George was the first to reach it, and when she got to the door she stopped, stunned. It was swinging open – and the Bolivian statue had gone!

She could only stammer, 'Ch – Ch – Chocabloc's not there!'

Equally horrified, Julian, Dick and Anne looked into the shed too.

'Then our alarm didn't go off!' said Dick. 'Or if it did, we never heard it.'

Timmy gave a little 'Woof!' and ran over to a small heap in the middle of the shed, just where Chocabloc had been standing the day before. 'Woof! Woof!' he repeated, as if he were pointing something out to them.

George went up to the dog, and saw that he was sniffing at the wrecked remains of what had been the alarm clock and the clever electrical device Julian had connected up to it. All the bits and pieces were twisted out of shape and mixed up together. There was a piece of paper lying beside them. George picked it up, read it, crumpled it up in disgust and dropped it again. But Julian, in his turn, picked it up and read the note out loud. It was written in block capitals with a ballpoint pen.

JUST TAKING THE STATUE FOR A LITTLE WALK! KIDS LIKE YOU LOT SHOULDN'T LEAVE THEIR NURSEMAIDS! NEXT TIME YOU GO POKING YOUR NOSES INTO OUR BUSINESS YOU'LL BE FOR IT, SO WATCH

OUT. MEANWHILE, IF YOU WANT TO KNOW THE TIME, BUY ANOTHER ALARM CLOCK. YOURS HAS HAD A SLIGHT ACCIDENT!

George was absolutely furious. Not only had the gangsters outwitted her and her cousins, they were laughing about it as well. 'And to think I wanted something to happen!' she growled. 'I suppose it serves me right! Well, they haven't heard the last of the Five yet. I'll find *some* way to catch those men.'

Then she thought of something that cheered her up a lot!

'Come to think of it,' she added, 'Kopak and his gang still haven't got the Inca Sun! I can just imagine their faces when they take the wooden breastplate off the statue and find the treasure has gone from its hiding place.'

'I bet Chuck and Luis will be in hot water!' said Dick, laughing.

Julian, however, was not laughing at all. 'What you *can* bet,' he pointed out, 'is that when Kopak finds the Inca Sun's missing, he'll guess who's responsible – and he'll come to make us tell him where it is.'

'Oh dear!' whispered Anne, going rather pale.

'We'd better let Barry know the latest developments,' George decided.

When the antique dealer had heard about the theft of his talking statue, he thought things over,

and said that he would go to the police and lay
a complaint against a person or persons unknown
for stealing it – still without mentioning the Inca
Sun. He didn't think there was much chance of
getting Chocabloc back, but if they didn't make
the expected moves, the gang would be suspicious.
'And when your father gets back, George, I'll tell
him the whole story,' he added, 'and we'll all go
to the police – and hope we've given them enough
evidence to arrest the thieves, if they haven't run
for it by then!'

As Barry himself admitted, he had a rather
carefree, happy-go-lucky temperament, and he had
forgotten about the danger that might threaten
himself and his young friends in the meantime.
However, he had a fascinating new subject on his
mind too! 'Guess what I had delivered today?' he
asked the children, looking very mysterious.

In fact, Anne guessed right at once. 'Not another
consignment of antiques from Bolivia?'

'Well done, Anne – how on earth did you know?
Yes: five very attractive statuettes, made of valuable
hardwood. 'I've only just unpacked them – come
and take a look! We'll examine them together.'

The five hardwood statuettes were very heavy.
'They aren't actually genuine antiques,' explained
Barry, 'but all the same they're very well made. Each
represents a different Bolivian god. The customers
like that sort of thing!'

Barry was so interested in the statuettes from a professional point of view that he seemed to be forgetting where they came from – and the mystery that might well surround them, too! It was left to Julian to point that out.

'Barry – are those statuettes a delivery you were expecting? Had you ordered them from somebody in Bolivia?' he asked.

'No, as a matter of fact I hadn't – so I was surprised to get them. Oh – I see what you mean!'

'Oh, quick!' cried George. 'Let's see if *they* have secret compartments in them too, like Chocabloc!'

Barry and the four cousins each picked up a statuette and examined it closely. They weighed them in their hands, shook them, tapped them, studied them through Barry's magnifying glass. Julian was the first to let out a cry of triumph.

'I say – the ear of this one moves!' he exclaimed. 'Watch this!'

And he twisted the little statue's ear. It came unscrewed like a kind of stopper, revealing a hollow space inside the statuette's head. Twelve magnificent emeralds fell out!

Barry uttered an exclamation of amazement as he looked at the jewels. Then he said, in hushed tones, 'I'm almost sure those gems have been removed from very old, rare pieces of jewellery. You can tell from the way they've been cut. I'll bet the gang that's been looting South American museums has something to do with this. Let's look at the other statuettes.'

And the ears of the other four little gods unscrewed too! Soon there was a whole pile of precious stones lying on Barry's table. The children looked at their friend.

'Barry,' said George solemnly. 'I think you'd better be ready for some uninvited visitors. This is the *second* time goods have come here by mistake. And they're obviously stolen goods too! The gang will want their loot back – you must take great care.'

'I must say, it's a pretty badly organised gang!' remarked Barry, with a smile. 'They may be good at looting museums and getting their haul past the Customs, but when it comes to delivering packages, their system definitely slips up!'

'The packaging!' cried George. 'Barry, we must look at it! At least this time we've got a real clue to lay our hands on!'

'Hands? Nose, more likely!' said Barry with a laugh, pointing at Timmy.

Sure enough, the intelligent dog was busy sniffing at a crate and some wrapping paper piled in a corner of the room behind the shop, just as if he knew what it was all about.

'You can smell something wrong, can you, Timmy? asked George, smiling. 'Right, let's have a look.'

She bent over the label on the crate, read it, and cried, 'I guessed right! We *have* got a clue now.

Look! The address just says Antique Shop, High Street, *Firrin*, England! You see? Whoever sent the statuettes from Bolivia meant them to go to Firrin, not Kirrin!'

'But the crate came here instead!' said Anne.

'That explains it all, agreed Julian.

'It may explain it all to you!' said Barry. 'But I'm still in the dark. All right, the sender wrote an F instead of a K, but I don't see how that gets us any farther.'

'That's because you're new to these parts,' said Dick. 'You see, there really *is* a village called Firrin, only a few miles away! It's quite a small place, but very likely someone's opened an antique shop there for the summer holiday-makers, just as you did in Kirrin. So it wasn't the *sender* who got the address wrong, it was the men delivering it who misread the label, or read it too quickly. You see, the address doesn't mention the name of the shop-keeper, and *your* shop is already well known hereabouts, so I expect they just thought the crate must be for you and brought it straight here – and the same thing happened once before, with Chocabloc! I'm certain that's it!'

Julian was looking very excited too. 'I say!' he cried. 'That address gives us a wonderful clue! All we have to do now is go to Firrin and take a look at any antique shop in the High Street there.'

'We'll cycle there directly after lunch!' George decided.

'You will be careful, won't you?' said Barry, sounding worried. '*Very* careful!'

'Oh yes, we promise we will,' said Anne, smiling nicely at him.

9

Firrin Village

Joan had cooked the children her extra-specially good hotpot for lunch, and they all did justice to it. It was very filling, so they could only manage a little ice cream and fruit salad for pudding, and they felt glad they were going to have some exercise cycling to Firrin!

Firrin was about half an hour's ride away, a little village nestling in a valley between two hills. Since it was a hot day, George decided she'd spare poor Timmy's paws and give him a ride for once – he sat happily in a basket fixed behind her saddle, enjoying himself very much!

Once they reached Firrin, the children planned to scout around inconspicuously. To avoid being noticed, they began by splitting up, and each of them came into the village's High Street a different way. It was easy to spot the antique shop, which looked small and rather dirty. There was all sorts of old junk standing outside the door. It didn't seem as if the owner had many customers, if any!

George had remembered to bring a pair of binoculars with her, and she raised them to her eyes and trained them on the shop for a better look, keeping in the cover of an old water butt standing by the roadside. Almost at once she saw a man come out of the shop and start looking for something or other among the junk. That must be the antique dealer.

'I say, I don't like the look of *him*!' she whispered to Timmy. 'He's squat, like a nasty toad, and he looks very brutal, with those hard, bright eyes!'

At that moment the man called out, loud enough for her to hear, 'Give me a hand with this, Chuck!'

'Coming, Mr Kopak!'

And out of the shop came the husky, big man George already knew so well! Now there could be no doubt about it – the Firrin antique shop was the gang's hideout!

George was just putting her binoculars back in their case when she saw a third man cross the road to join the other two: Luis, looking as elegant as ever, and distinctly out of place in this shabby village street.

When they had finished exploring, the Five met back at the spot where they had left their bicycles in a dry ditch. Julian and Dick, watching from different vantage points, had seen much the same as George. Anne, in her own quiet way, had done even better. Pretending that she wanted to buy a reel of cotton from the little haberdasher's shop, she had got into conversation with the kind woman serving her, and discovered the names of the two men who helped Mr Kopak run his antiques business. They were called Luis Perez and Chuck Baker!

'And the woman in the haberdasher's told me that Mr Kopak has lots of antiques delivered, but hardly any customers come to buy them,' said Anne in her soft voice. 'Not many summer holiday-makers or tourists get to this village at all, because it's such an out-of-the-way sort of place. In fact she said the local people feel quite sorry for "that poor man with the antique shop", and wonder what on earth he lives on.'

'*We* could tell them!' said George. 'He's got a nice little business going, all right – but we'll soon see about putting a stop to that!'

The children mounted their bicycles again and hurried back to Kirrin, feeling very pleased with the results of their expedition. They pedalled along with a will.

'Hello, children!' said Barry, as they rode up to his shop. 'Any luck?'

'A resounding success all along the line!' Dick told him. And George described what they had seen and found out in Firrin.

'So you were right!' said Barry. 'Well, now you've

found the gang's hideout, I think it really *is* time to go to the police.'

But George still didn't want to. 'What proof have we got to incriminate those men?' she asked. 'Oh no, Barry, don't let's go to the police yet! We want to know a little more about their activities first, and catch them red-handed if possible.' She glanced at her cousins, and said, 'We could go back to Firrin and make some more inquiries after it gets dark this evening. It'll be easier by night.'

'You'll do no such thing – or not on your own, anyway,' said Barry. 'I feel responsible for you children, and I don't want you cycling that distance after dark! We'll *all* go, in my station wagon – and if any action has to be taken, I'll take it, understand?'

George and Dick were not too pleased, but Julian seemed quite happy with this arrangement, so George thought it would be better not to protest, though she told herself she was going to do exactly as she wanted when they got to Firrin.

Meanwhile, Dick was giving the antique dealer the benefit of his own ideas on the whole subject! 'Have you ever stopped to wonder why the thieves didn't just come and say Chocabloc had been delivered to your shop by mistake?' he asked. 'Well, I think *I* know why, and it's simple – if you'd already suspected anything, they wouldn't have wanted to give away their own address, and it would have attracted attention to them. The same thing with the five little statuettes you've just had delivered! They'd rather steal them than ask for them back!'

'And *I* think,' said Julian, 'it was as another safeguard that the goods from Bolivia were sent just to "The Antique Shop", and the address didn't mention Kopak's name.'

'What's more,' added George, 'I wouldn't be surprised if the thieves came looking for those little statuettes this very night, so perhaps you'd better stay at home, Barry!'

The antique dealer smiled. 'Oho! I see what you're getting at, George! You don't want me on your expedition to Firrin tonight. Sorry, but the answer's the same as before. I'm not letting you run such a risk on your own. As for the statuettes, I doubt if they'll be in any great danger for another two or three days – not until the gang realise their goods have been delivered to the wrong place yet again. What's more, if they *do* come here to steal them, all they can take is the empty containers. Those amazing jewels are going straight off to join the Inca Sun in its bank vault!'

Secretly, George was disappointed, but she was a good sport, and couldn't help laughing. Well, it was just too bad! If Barry insisted on coming with them, she might as well give in with a good grace. And there'd be some advantages in going to Firrin by car. They'd save time, and it would be less tiring than cycling.

George was also thinking what a good thing it was that her parents were away! Uncle Quentin wouldn't have liked the children to go out so late at night. But it would be easy enough to get past dear old Joan, who didn't like the hot weather. It made her feel tired, and she liked to go to bed early.

So at dusk, the four cousins got on their bikes and rode off to Kirrin to meet Barry. The antique dealer was waiting for them. The children left their bicycles at his shop, and climbed into his station wagon. He started off straightaway.

When they reached Firrin, Barry parked the station wagon just outside the village, and told his passengers, 'Now, you kids be good! Wait here for me while I reconnoitre – and when I come back we'll decide what to do next, depending on circumstances.'

Anne was about to say, 'All right', out loud, but George squeezed her arm to make her keep quiet. Barry went off into the dark.

'Phew!' said Dick. 'Well, he didn't make us *promise* anything!'

'Just as I was hoping!' said George. 'I don't like to feel my hands are tied when the moment for action comes.'

'But – but you're not going to disobey Barry, are you?' said Anne timidly.

'That depends!' said George. 'It depends on circumstances, just as Barry said himself.'

'Only in an emergency, Anne,' Julian told his little sister, being cautious as usual.

As it happened, Julian as well as George thought it *was* an emergency when an hour had passed, and Barry still hadn't come back.

'I'm sure something's happened to him,' said George. 'We'd better go and see.'

The Five crept silently down the High Street of the sleeping village. But after a while they saw a shadow moving away from a wall. It came towards them – Barry, safe and sound.

'Hello – is that you?' he asked in an undertone. 'What are you doing out of the van?'

'Well, we didn't actually promise to stay in it!' George reminded him mischievously. 'Have you been keeping watch on the antique shop, or something?'

'Yes, and it's been very interesting too! Our friends have just left in a van – goodness knows what they're up to at this time of night!'

George didn't hesitate for a moment. 'This is our chance!' she cried. 'Let's get into their place and see if we can find Chocabloc!'

Barry and Julian both stared at her in surprise. 'George, do you really mean that?' said Barry. 'Surely you're not planning to break into Kopak's shop?'

George laughed. 'Well, not break in exactly,' she said. 'But the best guarded of fortresses often have one weak point! I bet that even if the front door's locked and the iron shutter is down over the display window, the gang will still have left a door or window unfastened somewhere round at the back. We can just look, can't we?'

Julian and even Anne might be very sensible for their age – Barry, on the other hand, was still young at heart for *his* age, and could be tempted by the idea of an adventure like this! He rather liked George's idea, and though he objected a bit it was only half-heartedly. In the end he agreed that they could at least go round to the back of the building. After all, the men had driven off, so there wasn't much risk.

'There seem to be a couple of outhouses or sheds, and a garage,' said George. 'Let's split up into two groups, with one going round each side. We'll join up again behind the shop. Barry, you go to the right with Julian and Anne, and I'll go to the left with Dick and Timmy.' Everyone was happy enough with this arrangement. 'Come on, quick!' George said to her cousin Dick. 'Let's not waste any more time – we don't know when the gangsters may be coming back.'

They rattled the door of a little shed beside the shop, but it was well and truly locked. Followed by Timmy, the two cousins went round the corner and found themselves facing another door – a door in a wall this time. It too was well locked, but the wall was not very high. It looked as if it surrounded a kind of yard. The antique dealer probably dumped crates and other rubbish there.

Dick and George exchanged meaning glances in the moonlight. 'Give me a leg up, then!' said George.

Dick immediately stood with his back to the wall, linked his hands, and gave George her 'leg up'. In a moment or so she had hauled herself up on top of the wall, and then dropped soundlessly and nimbly to the other side. A couple of seconds later she was pulling back the bolt that closed the door in the wall – and Dick and Timmy made their way into enemy territory too!

'So here we are inside – and we didn't have to break in either!' said George, grinning. 'Now, let's hurry up and search this yard. I wonder if we can find Chocabloc? If we can just lay hands on him – '

' – we'll be glad we've got Barry with us!' said Dick, finishing her sentence for her. 'That statue's a tremendous weight. Can you imagine us cycling off with a Bolivian idol over our handlebars, if we'd come by bike as you planned? We'd have had to saw him up first!'

Suddenly Dick stopped. George, who was cautiously making her way across the yard, had just stopped herself, and was pointing to something on the ground.

'Look at that, Dick! You've got very near to what actually happened! If that isn't poor old Chocabloc, sawn up into chunks, I'll eat my hat!'

'You haven't got a hat!' said Dick, but he bent over the pile of wood in front of him. George was right! He recognised the idol's big feet. They had made a kind of pedestal for the rest of the talking statue. The mask-like head had been split from top to bottom, and he saw bits of the polished wood of the body, and the wooden sun-ray breastplate too. The Inca god had been sawn up into pieces! Looking more closely, Dick realised that the gang had tried to burn the idol too. It was charred in several places. But the wood was very hard, and they hadn't been able to burn it completely.

'So now we know!' said George. 'Chocabloc's here all right – in pieces! The gangsters found out there was nothing inside him, after all, so then they tried to dispose of him, but no luck!'

Leaving the charred remains of Chocabloc where they had found them, George and Dick hurried off to join Barry, Julian and Anne, and tell them what they had found. Much to the children's delight, Barry didn't seem in a hurry to go to the police about this new development, although he was very indignant. 'What vandals!' he said. 'All right, that statue wasn't really my property after all, but they had no right to go destroying such a fine work of art! I'm going to get them myself for that!'

'Listen, Barry,' said Julian, soberly, 'you must expect that they'll attack your shop in some way, now they've made sure the idol is empty! In fact, I wonder if they may be there at this very moment, looking for the Inca Sun, and perhaps the statuettes too.'

However, Julian needn't have worried about that. When Barry and the children arrived back at the Kirrin Antique Shop, all was quiet and undisturbed, just as they had left it.

Except for an envelope which had been slipped through the front door, addressed to Mr Barry Lane.

10

Where are the Police?

'Oh, quick, Barry – open it!' said Anne. 'I'm sure it's from Kopak and his friends.'

'Huh!' snorted Barry. 'Too scared to face me, so they write a letter!'

He opened the envelope. The message it contained was made up of printed letters cut from newspaper and pasted on a sheet of white notepaper. He read it out loud.

'If you and those kids you're so friendly with don't give back our five statuettes and the Inca Sun, you'd better all watch out! Bring the goods down to the beach below Clifftops Manor at two a.m. tomorrow night. And don't go to the police, or you'll be sorry! Be there on your own.'

There was no signature.

'The beach below Clifftops Manor,' murmured George. 'Oh, I know where that is – why, it's directly opposite Kirrin Island!' Kirrin Island, a small island just off the mainland, had been in George's family for ages, and a little while before her mother and father had given it to her as her very own property.

'Yes, but that doesn't get us very much farther,' Dick said. 'Time's short – tomorrow night will soon be here! What can we do?'

'To start with,' said Barry angrily, 'we can make sure they don't get their hands on the Inca Sun *or* the precious stones. They're staying just where they are – in the bank vault!'

'I've got an idea!' announced George.

'Never!' said Dick, pretending to be surprised. 'George, you astonish me! Come on, out with it – we're all listening!'

'It's very simple. Barry goes to meet the crooks and says he doesn't know anything about the Inca Sun. He tells them the statue was stolen from him and that's all he knows. And then he can give them back the statuettes, but not the precious stones, of course! We can get some bits of coloured glass and put them inside the container spaces instead.'

'Do you think that'll take the gangsters in?' said Julian, looking doubtful.

'Wait a minute, Ju – I haven't finished yet! While *he's* talking to them, *we'll* keep watch on the beach from a distance. And *then* we call in the police, just at the crucial moment – because Barry will have given them warning beforehand so that they're lying in wait to catch the thieves!'

'What?' said Dick – in genuine surprise this time. 'George, I never thought I'd hear *you* suggest calling in the police!'

'That will be the right time to do it, Dick, you idiot! We want the police to catch the men red-handed, threatening Barry and demanding the jewels!'

Barry and even the sensible Julian thought this was a good plan, and as for Anne, she heaved a sigh of relief. After tomorrow night, this adventure would be all over!

They agreed that Barry would go to the police station and explain everything some time during the course of the day. However, it so happened that he had a positive flood of tourists in his shop nearly all the time, and he was far too busy to fit in a visit to the police station. By evening, when at last he could shut the shop, he felt it was too late to go to the police in person – for one thing he was expecting the children to arrive any moment, with the mock 'jewels' they had promised to get hold of during the day. So he rang up the police instead, explained that they would have a wonderful chance, that night, of capturing three of the members of the gang that had been looting South American museums. All they had to do was lie in wait around the beach below Clifftops Manor.

Barry told his story fast, and in a rather excited manner – after all, it *was* an exciting story! It also sounded a very improbable story to the Inspector at the other end of the line. He immediately thought that his caller must be a practical joker. It so happened that the Inspector had been the victim of a similar practical joke quite recently, and he genuinely thought a hoaxer was trying to pull his leg again and get the police to turn out for nothing in the middle of the night! The Inspector had a good sense of humour himself, so he thought that rather than lose his temper and shout, he'd enter into the spirit of the thing.

'Oh, splendid!' he told Barry, in enthusiastic tones. 'That's fine, then – we'll be stationed round the beach at two in the morning! You can count on us. See you later, then!'

And he put the receiver down, chuckling to himself.

Barry was glad the Inspector had got the idea so quickly – somehow, he'd rather expected he would be asked to do a little more explaining! But he was able to tell the children that all was well when they arrived a few moments later, and they all set to work to pack the gleaming bits of coloured glass inside the heads of the five statuettes.

They were at their posts at a quarter to two in the morning. The children had set off first, and were there a good half-hour early, in hiding behind some gorse bushes among the sand dunes. They had a very good view of the beach, so they could see Barry when he arrived, carrying a suitcase which they knew contained the statuettes. The antique dealer started pacing up and down the beach, because there was quite a chilly breeze. Barry wasn't at all scared. After all, he was sure there was a squad of policemen stationed in hiding round the beach to protect him!

At two o'clock precisely, Dick nudged his cousin George. 'Look – there's a boat coming in from the sea!'

George had been watching the path and the dunes, wondering if she could make out the shapes of any policemen. She turned round – sure enough, a boat was making for the beach. She hadn't thought that the crooks themselves might come by sea. Would the police have their own motor launch handy?

They could just hear the sound of the boat's engine. Barry had stopped pacing, and he too was looking at the boat. It came in to land, and two men jumped out on the beach. By the light of the moon, the children recognised Luis and Chuck.

'There they are!' whispered Anne. 'Oh, I do hope the policemen are here!'

'Ssh!' said Julian. 'Of course they are!'

The wind blowing in off the sea carried the sound of voices to the children.

'Got the goods?' asked Chuck.

'Here you are,' said Barry, handing them his suitcase. Luis put it down on the ground, opened it, and looked at the contents by the light of a torch.

'Yes, the statuettes are here,' he said, 'but where's the Inca Sun?'

Barry looked innocent. 'I've no idea what you're talking about!' he said.

'Oh yes, you have! We got that wooden idol back, but the Sun wasn't in its hiding place!'

'What sun? What hiding place?'

Chuck took hold of Barry's arm. 'Don't you fool around with us! If you're not gonna play, we're taking you to see the boss!'

'Look here, what are you after?' protested Barry. 'I don't understand.'

'Then you can come on board the yacht and find out more!' said Luis. 'Into the boat – come on! The yacht's standing out to sea.'

And the two men forced poor Barry into the motor boat that had brought them ashore. Barry was thinking it was about time for the police to step in, and perhaps he ought to prompt them! 'Help!' he shouted. 'Help, I'm being kidnapped!'

He expected to see lots of policemen rush out of hiding – but nothing at all happened. In horror and dismay, he realised nothing *was* going to happen! He had to obey the two men.

They were laughing. 'Shout as much as you like – nobody will hear!' they said.

As for the children, they had to watch, stunned and powerless, as their friend was taken away. Why didn't the police intervene? 'I can't make it out!' said Julian, puzzled. 'Can Barry have forgotten to tell the police after all? No – he told us he had! I know he's a bit scatterbrained, but I wouldn't have thought he was *that* bad!'

However, there it was – the facts had to be faced! The gangsters had kidnapped Barry, the police had not come to his aid after all, and now he was in real trouble.

'We must *do* something!' said Dick.

'What can we do? We're only children!' said Anne miserably, shivering. 'Oh, poor Barry!'

'Well, moaning and grizzling won't get us any-where. We must act!' said George. 'And I've got an idea!'

Dick smiled – not sarcastically, for once. 'Glad to hear it,' was all he said. 'Come on, we're all listening!'

George's plan was a bold one, and typical of George herself. She pointed to a dark shape standing motionless in the middle of the bay. 'That must be the yacht they mentioned, with Kopak on board. Now, we're quite close to home here, so let's hurry back to Kirrin Cottage and fetch my rowing boat. Under cover of the dark, we can get close to the yacht without being noticed if we're careful not to make any noise.'

'And then what?' asked Dick.

'We'll have to decide what to do next when we get there – come on, quick!'

Soon afterwards, George's rowing boat, with Julian and George herself at the oars, was silently approaching the yacht anchored out in the bay. She was lying quite low in the water, and when the rowing boat came alongside her George realised it would be quite easy to get on board. She listened, but could not hear any sound. 'I'm going aboard – coming with me, Dick?' she whispered.

The two cousins nimbly clambered up on the deck of the yacht. There was nobody in sight – what luck! However, they could hear voices coming up through a hatch. Going very quietly, Dick and George went closer to it.

'He claims he never set eyes on the Inca Sun, Mr Kopak!' Chuck was saying.

'And we ought to have found the precious stones inside those statuettes, but they're fakes!' added Luis.

'Ah. In other words,' said another, harsh voice, which must belong to Kopak, 'you're trying to palm a few bits of coloured glass off on us, and the Sun is shining somewhere else! So how do you explain that, young man?'

'I don't have to explain anything!' said Barry firmly. 'I haven't the faintest idea what you're talking about. Ever since that wretched Bolivian

statue came my way, people have been after me –
I've been threatened, robbed, and now kidnapped.
There's no sense in it at all!'

Kopak's voice sounded menacing now. 'If you're
not careful, young man, I personally shall find ways
to refresh your memory! Either you tell me where
the Inca Sun is, or I strangle you slowly – like
this . . .'

The gangster must have been putting his words
into practice, because Dick and George suddenly
heard the horrible sound of a faint moan. They went
very pale.

'We can't just stand here listening to this!'
said Dick softly. 'Let's get down there and rescue
Barry!'

'What, the two of us – two children, against three
grown men?'

The moan died away, and they heard Kopak's
voice again. 'Was that enough for you? Are you
going to talk, or shall I start again? I may squeeze
a little harder this time!'

'Please – I don't know anything!' gasped Barry.

'Dick, I know what to do,' breathed George.
'Promise to do whatever I say!'

'But I – '

'Listen, old chap, I haven't got time to explain!
It's too urgent. Go back to the boat, quick – I want
you and Julian to set off at once to swim to my
island.'

'Swim to Kirrin Island?' said Dick, baffled.

'Yes, I know the water isn't very warm, and it's about two-thirds of a mile to go – but you can do that. And I must have the boat left here because I'll be needing it. Anne and Timmy are to wait for me in the boat.'

'But what are you going to *do*, George?'

'I tell you, there isn't time to explain now. Just listen to me! Once you and Julian are on the island, go and hide down in the castle dungeons – by the door into the north dungeon!'

'The one with the huge, heavy wooden door?'

'That's right. We're going to try imprisoning the gangsters there!'

'But how are you going to get them to the island in the first place?' asked Dick.

'Leave that to me! The vital thing is for you and Julian to be there ready to slam the door. It takes more than one person to move it fast, and I'd never get it shut in time on my own, but the three of us should be able to do it – and meanwhile the gangsters will be inside looking for an imaginary treasure! Now, do hurry!'

Another moan drifted up through the hatch, and George gave her cousin a little push to start him on his way. Then she took several deep breaths. She knew she must be absolutely relaxed to play the part she'd decided on. Right! Now she was ready!

Boldly, and without trying to muffle the sound

of her footsteps any longer, she hurried down the hatchway. She saw light shining underneath a doorway, pushed the door open, and marched into the cabin beyond it.

A painful scene met her eyes. Chuck was grinning broadly and Luis was scowling, while Kopak, the Firrin 'antique dealer', was slowly tightening his powerful hands round Barry Lane's neck. Barry was tied to a chair.

'*Now* will you talk?' growled Kopak.

'Stop it!' cried George.

11

George the Actress

The three men swung round, and Kopak let go of his victim. George didn't give them time to recover from their surprise. She threw herself dramatically at Kopak's feet, raising pleading hands to him while tears ran down her cheeks.

'Please, sir, don't! Don't hurt Mr Lane! I heard what you were saying about the Inca Sun – he doesn't know anything about it, it was me – oh, you've half strangled him!'

She leapt to her feet and ran across to Barry as if she wanted to look more closely at his bruised neck – and seized her chance to whisper in his ear, 'Back me up, Barry, and whatever I say, don't be surprised!' Then she said, out loud, 'Oh, this is terrible! Please, *please* untie him!'

Kopak had pulled himself together now. 'Who on earth *is* this boy?' he growled.

'I'm a girl, not a boy,' said George, 'and I

won't have you hurting my friend Mr Lane any more!'

Chuck and Luis exchanged glances of amusement. Oh, so she was a girl, was she? Then it wasn't surprising she was weeping so noisily and grovelling on the floor!

However, Kopak was frowning suspiciously. 'How did you get here, little girl?' he asked.

George began sobbing again, burying her face in her hands as if she were too upset to talk. Barry was beginning to get his breath back. All this was most un-George-like behaviour! He guessed she was only acting a part, trying to play for time.

'Oh – oh – oh, please sir!' she sobbed. But while she wept, George was busily working out just how long it would take Dick and Julian to reach her island. They were both very strong swimmers. 'Oh – oh, *please* set Mr Lane free! He hasn't done anything!'

'Kid, I asked you a question! If you're going to be as obstinate as your friend here, you'd better watch your step!'

George let out a very lifelike and horrible shriek of terror, and turned as if to run to the cabin door. But Luis stood in her way.

'You answer the boss's question! How did you get here?'

'Oh – oh, I was playing pirates with my little cousin Anne! We came out after dark, just to show the boys we weren't scared, you see, and we borrowed my father's rowing boat without telling anyone.' She looked miserable, and sniffled. 'And then the current carried us away, and I couldn't row any more, so I tied the boat up to the chain of your anchor, and I climbed on board to look for help, and then I heard Mr Lane's voice and – '

'And you felt curious, so you eavesdropped, right?'

'Oh – oh, please, I couldn't help it, sir!'

'This little girl is one of those brats from the house where Lane left the idol,' said Luis.

'Well, well, well!' said Kopak, looking hard at George. 'In that case, since your friend here won't talk, and you say he doesn't know anything, I suppose you *do* know something! Did you and your little friends by any chance find a large piece of jewellery inside that wooden statue?'

George looked confused, hung her head, and shifted about as if she felt very uneasy. But really she was delighted. Everything was going just the way she wanted!

'Oh, so you won't reply? You want me to start strangling your friend Lane again? Right here in front of you?'

George looked horrified. 'No, no!' she cried. 'I'll tell you everything, sir. My friends and I – well, we knocked the idol over, and it broke. And there was something very pretty inside, shining like – like the sun!'

Kopak exchanged glances with his accomplices. 'Ah, now we're getting somewhere!' he said. 'So that's it, eh? You had no scruples about stealing this pretty thing from Lane! Unfortunately, it just so happens that the Inca Sun is *our* property. And you'd better let us have it back at once.'

George seemed to be in a state of terror. 'Yes – yes, of course, sir! We hid it on Kirrin Island – that's quite close!'

'And how about those bits of worthless glass I found in the statuettes? Do you know anything about *them*?' He showed her one of the little statues.

Barry had been beginning to feel hopeful, but his heart sank again. If George told Kopak she was responsible for replacing the jewels in the statuettes with coloured glass too, he'd never believe her story. However, she was too clever for that! 'Those statuettes?' she said, as if puzzled. 'Oh, we were at Mr Lane's shop when they arrived, and we helped him put them in the window, but I didn't know they had anything inside them!'

'Nor did I!' put in Barry. 'That's why I couldn't understand what you were going on about.'

'Hm,' Kopak looked shaken. With any luck, he was beginning to wonder if the jewels had been stolen and replaced by worthless coloured glass back in Bolivia, before they were ever sent to

England. 'Hm – well, let's forget the statuettes for the moment. You say the Inca Sun is hidden on this island, eh? Chuck, go and make sure this little girl wasn't lying about her boating expedition, will you? Tie her boat up well to our stern – and bring her little cousin on board.'

'Be careful,' George warned Chuck. 'My dog's in the boat too. I'd better come with you, or he might bite you.'

Five minutes later, Anne and Timmy were clambering on board the yacht. Anne was terrified, but she smiled bravely at George, who guessed she was trying to tell her, without any words, that Julian and Dick had swum off to Kirrin Island. Anne only hoped George's plan would work!

When they were back in the cabin with Barry, Luis and Kopak, the boss of the gang turned to George again.

'I hope for your sake you were telling us the truth about the Inca Sun! Okay, Chuck,' he added, 'raise anchor and start the engine. We're going over to that island to pick up our treasure!'

George had difficulty in hiding her glee. Thanks to her cunning trick, she had led the gangsters to do just as she wanted. It was quite an intoxicating feeling to be manipulating Kopak, Luis and Chuck like so many puppets!

However, if the drama was to go on unfolding in the way she'd planned, they didn't want to arrive at the island too soon. She needed time for Julian and Dick to get into position.

'You must be careful,' said George, sounding alarmed. 'There are sharp rocks round the island, and you can't land just anywhere. I know these waters very well, sir.'

'Then you can guide us in! But don't forget that if you try to escape, your cousin and your friend Lane will pay for it – understand?'

It didn't take the yacht long to get to the island, and in fact George had been telling the truth about the sharp, underwater rocks which made landing there risky. Kopak told his accomplices to drop anchor some way out to sea.

'Now,' he told Chuck and Luis, 'you take the boat and go and get the Inca Sun. The little girl will guide you. I'll wait here with the other two prisoners.'

George bit her lip. She hadn't foreseen that Kopak would stay on board! Well, that was just too bad – they'd have to deal with him separately. She was sorry to leave Anne, Timmy and Barry behind, but she had to get into the boat with Luis and Chuck.

'I must look for the place where you can come in safely and pull a boat up on shore,' she told the two men. 'It isn't easy in the dark.' She made them go slowly all round the island – hoping that Julian and Dick, who must have arrived by now, would hear the sound and hurry down to the dungeons if they weren't already there.

'Look, there it is!' she said at last. 'A tiny cove with a little beach!'

Chuck brought the boat in, and its keel scraped over the sand. The gangsters and George landed. 'Now where?' asked Luis.

'We hid the Sun in that ruined old castle you can see up there above us,' George told the men. They looked the way she was pointing, and saw the impressive ruins of the castle on Kirrin Island – they weren't to know it actually belonged to this little girl, and she knew every stone of it like the back of her hand!

'Not a bad hiding place,' said Luis. 'Well, you go ahead, kid, and show us the way.'

In single file, the three of them set off along the narrow path leading up to the rocky mound where the castle had been built. The moon shone down on the trees and bushes and the grassy space in front of the ruins. George went in under a stone archway, crossed a courtyard paved with broken flagstones, and entered a huge, dilapidated hall.

'We're not quite there yet,' said George. 'Follow me!' Actually, she was leading them by a very roundabout way, just to confuse them – but at last she came to the big flagstone with the iron ring in it that covered the entrance to the dungeons. 'There's a sort of well-shaft under that,' she explained, 'and when my cousins and I were playing here we climbed down the iron ladder inside, and found the dungeons at the bottom. That's where we hid the Sun!'

Chuck heaved the stone up. 'You go first and show us the way!' he said.

The ladder went down and down into the ground, but George was nimble as a cat, and she climbed down easily, shining a torch that Luis handed her so that the men could see the way they were going.

'I hope Dick and Julian can hear us coming,' thought George. 'Poor things, they must be terribly cold in their wet clothes! I just hope they don't sneeze or anything.'

Dick and Julian were in position, lurking in the shadows beside the great wooden door to the underground dungeon. Suddenly they saw a light bobbing about, and they could make out the figures of George, Luis and Chuck behind it.

'It's a pity Mr Kopak didn't come too, instead of staying on the yacht,' said George to the gangsters – that was to let her cousins know the third man wasn't with them after all. 'He'd have liked this place, I expect.'

'Never mind the light banter, just carry on walking!' grunted Chuck.

'We're there. It's in that room ahead – we buried the Sun at the back of the room, under a stone in the left-hand corner.'

As she spoke, George stood back to let the gangsters go first. She was hoping Chuck and Luis would be in such a hurry to lay hands on the treasure that they wouldn't bother her any more, and would rush straight into the dungeon. After all, they didn't think they had anything to fear from a little girl!

And her hopes were fulfilled! The two men strode right on into the dungeon. Standing in the doorway, George turned and saw Dick and Julian emerge from hiding.

'Now – quick!' she whispered.

Without a word, the three cousins flung all their weight against the huge, heavy door of the dungeon. It swung round and slammed shut with a tremendous crash. 'We've done it!' cried Dick, hearing muffled shouts of rage from the gangsters inside. 'They're trapped!' Quickly, they turned the key in the lock.

'They can shout as loud as they like in the dark there!' said Julian, grinning.

'Yes – they won't even have the Inca Sun to give them a bit of light!' said George happily. 'Now, let's hurry back up. Are you two frozen?'

'No, we're quite all right,' said Dick, following George up the well-shaft. 'We thought we'd better undress before we started our swim, and we tied our bundles of clothes on our heads. But where's Kopak?'

'And Anne?' asked Julian, bringing up the rear. 'And Barry and Timmy?'

'I'm afraid Kopak's still on board his yacht,

waiting for his accomplices to come back,' George explained. 'Anne and Barry and Timmy are there too!'

This was bad news to the two boys. Their little sister was in the power of the gangster boss – and they couldn't get at him! George came up out of the well-shaft, waited for her cousins to join her, and saw their gloomy faces. 'Don't look so miserable,' she said cheerfully. 'Everything will be all right! My plan's worked pretty well so far, except for a few details. We've put Luis and Chuck out of action, so now we only have to deal with Kopak, and the odds are on our side!'

'He's got hostages, remember!'

'If we act quickly enough he'll have to let them go,' said George confidently.

'What exactly are you planning to do?' asked Julian. He felt more hopeful now himself – his cousin's confidence had infected him!

'We'll take the boat back to the yacht as quietly as possible – luckily there are oars in it, so we can row. Then we must try to take Kopak by surprise and overpower him, and after that everything should go smoothly. We'll free Barry, Anne and Timmy and make for Kirrin – and then all the police will have to do is pick up Luis and Chuck from their dungeon. That is, *if* we can get the police to pay any attention *this* time!'

'The only thing is, Kopak may be up on deck

looking for the boat,' Dick pointed out. 'And if he spots Julian and me instead of Luis and Chuck, what shall we do about that?'

'That's a risk we just have to run – anyway, we've got no choice!'

As they discussed the situation, the three cousins had emerged from the ruins of the castle and were walking down the path to the little beach. Quickly, they got into the boat, and Julian and Dick took the oars. Once they were out of the little creek, the three of them looked for the yacht standing out to sea.

But however hard they peered, they couldn't see Kopak's vessel anywhere. The yacht had disappeared!

12

All Ends Well

George, Dick and Julian could hardly believe their eyes. This was not just a nasty surprise – it was a real disaster! 'I don't believe it!' said George at last. 'Kopak would never have gone off without the Inca Sun – not unless he had a very good reason.'

'And Anne, and Barry and Timmy are still with him!' said Julian in dismay.

'What on earth can have happened to the yacht?' asked Dick.

Of course, the three cousins couldn't know what had been happening on board the yacht since George left it. When Luis and Chuck had set out for the island with her, Anne, feeling very scared, was left alone with that horrible Kopak. Poor Barry was still tied to his chair, but at least it made the little girl feel rather better to have Timmy beside her.

'Very well,' Kopak told his prisoners. 'Now we wait. And for everyone's sake, let's hope my friends

come back with the Inca Sun! Then all we have
to do is take a closer look at that business of the
statuettes, and the jewels that ought to have been
inside them.'

Barry shrugged his shoulders, as if this meant
nothing to him. Anne, who knew very well that
the Inca Sun, with the Opal Sun inside it, wasn't
on the island at all, couldn't help shivering. Once
again, she hoped with all her heart that her brothers
and George would manage to get Chuck and Luis
out of the way – then they'd only have Kopak to
deal with. Oh, if only Barry wasn't tied up!

Kopak walked to the hatchway. 'I have to go up
on deck now, but don't you move, little girl, and
don't let that dog move either!' he said. 'I'll be back
in a couple of minutes.'

George had told Timmy to be a good dog and
wait for her – but he did hate being parted from
his mistress, and the least little signal from Anne
would have been quite enough to make him fling
himself at the gangster's throat – but Anne had the
sense to hold him back.

As soon as Kopak had gone out, however, she
hurried over to Barry and tried to untie him. 'Barry,
I *must* set you free!' she whispered. But the knots
were too tight for her little fingers. 'Oh dear – I
must do it!'

'It's no good, Anne. You'd need a knife, and we
haven't got one,' said Barry. 'Anyway, even if I was

free I wouldn't have much chance of overpowering that man. He's got a gun!'

Realising it was no use trying to free Barry, Anne at least did her best to cheer him up. 'You mustn't worry too much, you know,' she told him. 'George has a plan!'

'I thought so, the moment I saw her crying and carrying on like that – not at all like the George I know! What's she thought up?'

Quickly, Anne told him. 'George is awfully clever – well, you heard her! She made the gangsters think the Inca Sun was hidden on Kirrin Island, didn't she?'

'Yes – while it's really safe in the bank, along with the jewels out of those statuettes!' said Barry, smiling.

'But Chuck and Luis weren't to know that – and Julian and Dick are over on the island already, setting a trap for them! Then we'll only have Kopak to deal with!'

'And you haven't dealt with me yet, young lady!' said a furious voice.

In alarm, Barry and Anne glanced at the doorway – and saw Kopak standing there! The gangster was white with rage. He walked into the room with a heavy tread and shook his fist under the antique dealer's nose.

'Oh yes, I heard all that! You were pretending to be innocent, but you have the jewels sitting in your bank. As for *you*,' he added, turning to the terrified Anne, 'you and your little friends thought you could play games with me, did you?'

He raised his hand to slap Anne's face – but Timmy gave a low growl. Kopak wasn't really a very brave man, and he hastily retreated to the doorway.

'Well, I'm sure you won't mind a little wait!' he told his prisoners. 'If you thought you could get the better of me, you were making a big mistake! Too bad about Chuck and Luis – I'm not hanging around waiting for those brats to get back here! I shall make for the coast, and hold on to this little girl as a hostage while *you*, Mr Lane, take me to your bank as soon as it opens and withdraw the Sun and the other jewels from that vault you mentioned.'

Barry's eyes lit up – and Kopak laughed!

'I wouldn't advise you to try any tricks, either. Because *before* we leave for the bank, I shall take good care to hide the girl in a secret place known only to myself – and where she'll die of starvation if I don't come back to let her out. So you see, it wouldn't be very clever to go calling the police when we get the stuff out of the bank. I'm rather wilier than you thought! Ha, ha, ha!'

And the gangster went out, closing the door after him and leaving his prisoners in the cabin again.

Barry and Anne looked at each other in dismay. They had been hoping the other two men would be dealt with and George and the boys would soon be back to set them free, but now they were worse off than ever. Anne burst into tears.

'Don't cry, Anne,' Barry told her. 'After all, there's nothing so dreadful about it. Of course I'll have to give Kopak the Inca Sun and the other jewels, but we shall get out of this safe and sound, and that's all that really matters.'

'Oh, it's all my fault!' sobbed Anne. 'I was so silly – it's because of what I said we're in this mess. If only I'd kept my mouth shut! George will be furious. She'll never, never forgive me for ruining her plan, and the gang will get off scot free, all because of me! And the people robbing those museums in South America will never be arrested – how could I be so stupid?'

'You only told me George's plan to cheer me up, Anne, and that was very kind and thoughtful of you. *You* weren't to know Kopak was listening behind the door!'

Anne stopped crying with a sudden effort, wiped her eyes and raised her head defiantly. Whatever Barry said, she knew she *had* been silly – and now she felt it was up to her to put things right.

The little girl wasn't sure just *what* she could do, but she was ready to try anything. And suddenly the door opened and Kopak appeared again, this time with a pistol in his hand!

'We're making for the coast,' he told them. 'But

before we land I'm going to get rid of this dog –
he'll only be in the way!'

He was already aiming the gun at poor Timmy,
and Anne knew she had to act at once. 'Timmy –
get him!' she cried.

And before the gangster had time to fire, the dog
went for his throat. Kopak did fire the gun, but his
bullet buried itself in the cabin wall! He had to drop
the pistol to try to tear the dog away from him, and
Anne didn't waste any time. She ran to pick the
gun up. Pointing it at Kopak, she said, 'All right,
Timmy – good dog! Let go now! Sit!'

Rather regretfully, Timmy obeyed. The terrified
Kopak was gasping for breath.

'Now then, untie Mr Lane!' Anne told him, quite
fiercely. 'Quick! And be careful, or I'll fire!'

She was holding the gun in both hands, and
now Kopak was really frightened. It was obvious
that Anne knew very little about firearms, and
she might easily pull the trigger without even
meaning to. 'Here – take it easy, little girl!' he
croaked.

'Untie my friend!'

Kopak hurried to do as she said. He cut the cords
binding Barry with a knife. Feeling rather stiff, the
antique dealer stood up, rubbed his wrists, and then
took the pistol from Anne.

'Anne, you get that cord and tie Kopak's hands
behind his back, as tight as you can!' he said. 'As for

you, Kopak, you'd better not try struggling. Well done, Anne – good girl!'

Once Anne had tied the first knot, Barry finished the job of trussing the wretched man up. Then he put the pistol in his pocket and went up on deck, followed by Anne and Timmy.

'Good work, Anne!' he said. 'And you too, Timmy! Now all we have to do is turn round and go back in the direction of Kirrin Island.'

On the little beach of Kirrin Island, George and her cousins were staring gloomily out to sea. They couldn't think what to do next. Where were Anne, Barry and Timmy now?

Then, suddenly, George let out a cry of joy. She had just seen a moving shadow – the shape of the yacht, coming back. 'Quick!' she cried. 'Let's go to meet her – the first thing to do is get on board.' Of course, she thought Kopak was still in charge.

But when the little boat was close to the yacht, George and her cousins were amazed and delighted to hear familiar voices hailing them. 'George! Dick! Julian! Come on board!' shouted Barry.

'Oh, I'm so pleased to see you!' cried Anne.

'Woof! Woof!' barked Timmy.

'It's Barry and Timmy and Anne!' cried Dick. 'They're all right!'

A moment later, the Five and Barry Lane were all on the deck of the yacht, talking excitedly. But all of a sudden Timmy gave a ferocious snarl and leapt at something – Kopak had somehow managed to struggle free, and was furtively trying to clamber over the rail and make his escape by swimming away. However, Timmy wasn't having any of that! Firmly held in the dog's strong jaws, the gangster had to surrender, and Barry and the children tied him up again.

'Now let's get back to Kirrin as fast as we can!' said George happily.

As soon as they reached the village, Barry went to the police station with the Five and their prisoner. The Inspector he had spoken to the previous day was on duty himself – and when he heard their amazing story he could hardly believe his ears.

'Good gracious me!' he said. 'Then the SOS message I got yesterday wasn't a practical joke after all. Well! I'm very sorry, Mr Lane, I really am!'

'Never mind that now!' said Barry, good-humoured as usual. 'Here's the leader of the gang – and if you think he could do with a little company in the cells, just send your men over to the castle on Kirrin Island. They'll find his accomplices there, locked in a dungeon.'

Dawn was approaching, and the sky was getting light. The Inspector had soon made his arrangements. He called up a small squad of men, borrowed the local coastguard launch, and told the children they could come too and guide the police to the two gangsters.

George was delighted. Everything would be all right now! The three gangsters would soon be in jail – they'd be questioned, and she felt sure they'd give the police a lead to the Peruvian and Bolivian gangs who had been burgling all those museums in South America.

The launch came ashore in the little cove on Kirrin Island, and Timmy was the first to jump out on land, closely followed by George. They both dashed towards the ruins. Julian, Dick, Anne, and the Inspector and his men went after them.

Once they were at the bottom of the well-shaft they could all hear the muffled shouts of Luis and Chuck. 'Open this door! Let us out!'

George exchanged mischievous glances with her cousins. 'All right, if you say so!' she shouted back.

She turned the big key in the lock, and with the help of the boys, pulled the heavy door back. Then she walked into the dungeon herself, holding her torch. All the gangsters could see was the outline of her figure, and they thought she was alone, so they made a dash for her, shouting, 'Decided to let us out have you? You'll be sorry you played this trick on us!'

George was enjoying herself hugely. 'Will I?' she said. She stepped aside smartly – and Luis and Chuck walked straight into the arms of the policemen waiting in the dark outside. She heard handcuffs click round the gangsters' wrists.

'Now you've got all three of them!' said Dick happily.

'And we shan't be letting them get away in a hurry!' the Inspector told him. He, too, was very pleased they had caught these important criminals.

As for Chuck and Luis, they were furious! Everyone went back up into the daylight, and Barry and the children took deep breaths of the lovely fresh air. Timmy began scampering about after rabbits in the dewy grass. The sun had risen, and was bathing the old castle and the calm sea in its bright light.

They went back on board the launch and started out for the mainland. Barry was chuckling to himself, Julian and Dick kept smiling, and as for Anne, she was so pleased everything had turned out all right that she couldn't help laughing with delight!

George, however, was looking unexpectedly gloomy. Guessing there was something wrong, the faithful Timmy pushed his head lovingly into her hand, as if to say, 'I'm here and you can always count on me, so don't worry!'

Dragging herself away from her thoughts George patted him, and then sighed deeply.

Anne looked at her cousin. 'Whatever's the matter, George?' she asked sympathetically. 'You look worried.'

'I *am* worried!' said George, with deep feeling. 'I've just remembered something! My mother and father were coming back from their holiday first thing this morning – they're probably at Kirrin Cottage already, and they'll find we're not there and we haven't slept in our beds! My father will be simply furious! You know how strict he is, and he'll say it's all my doing, and I led the rest of you into trouble. I'm sure I'll be punished.'

The Inspector had overheard her, and he smiled. 'Don't worry, Miss Kirrin!' he told her. I've just sent a radio message back to the station, telling them there that we'd got our men, and asking them to ring your home and let your people know you were quite all right. I'll be surprised if you get much of a scolding!'

George thought that she wasn't so sure of that – so it was a lovely surprise when they came ashore and found Uncle Quentin and Aunt Fanny waiting, and smiling happily at them! George's father gave her a great big hug.

'Well done, George!' he said. 'You did splendidly – and so did all the rest of you! I really ought to be very angry with you – but I've had a lovely holiday, and I don't think I can bring myself to be cross just now. Let's go back to Kirrin Cottage! Luckily for Joan's peace of mind, the first she knew of your being out all night was when the police rang just now – and she's busy cooking you a huge breakfast.'

Next day the newspapers were full of the capture of the gangsters by the Five. They were interviewed on radio and television too! As for Barry Lane, he was getting lots of wonderful publicity out of the case – you could hardly get into his shop for all the tourists who wanted to buy things from him.

Meanwhile the police were very busy investigating the whole affair. Of course, Interpol had been informed. Kopak and his accomplices were prepared to tell them a great deal, hoping for a more lenient prison sentence if they did, so many members of the gangs who had been looting museums in South America were identified and tracked down, and the museums got nearly all their priceless treasures back.

And a little while later, the children got a huge and mysterious package. When they undid it, they found that it had been sent by the La Paz museum as a token of appreciation. It was a wooden reproduction of their old friend Chocabloc!

'We can put it up in the garden, like a totem pole!' said Julian.

'Yes,' agreed George. 'Our very own totem – and it will always remind us of the case of the Inca God!'